KU-682-611

# Guns Along the Gila

When he finds the struggling Wheatley family trying to make it all by themselves through troubled Apache territory of the Sonora Desert, army scout John Best begs them to wait for him to guide them. But they set out on their own and the Apaches strike first.

Now Best finds himself helping the teenager Lucien to rescue his beautiful sister Emma from a terrible fate. However the US Cavalry, under a demented newly-commissioned officer, seems to be determined to complicate matters instead of riding to the rescue. It's all down to Best to fight his way through despite the odds.

*By the same author*

Apache Country
Carnigan's Claim
Mogollon Rim Rider
Tombstone Lullaby

# Guns Along the Gila

## WALT MASTERSON

A Black Horse Western

ROBERT HALE · LONDON

© Walt Masterson 2007
First published in Great Britain 2007


ISBN 978-0-7090-8478-5

Robert Hale Limited
Clerkenwell House
Clerkenwell Green
London EC1R 0HT

www.halebooks.com

The right of Walt Masterson to be identified as
author of this work has been asserted by him
in accordance with the Copyright, Designs and
Patents Act 1988

| KENT LIBRARIES AND ARCHIVES | |
| --- | --- |
| C153329071 | |
| HJ | 18/01/2008 |
| | £11.99 |
| | |

Typeset by
Derek Doyle & Associates, Shaw Heath
Printed and bound in Great Britain by
Antony Rowe Limited, Wiltshire

*For my daughter, Melanie Eve,*
*who wears a mean pair of chaps.*

# CHAPTER ONE

The Apaches had been trailing John Best all morning, and he knew they were catching up faster than they should have been. The Sonoran Desert badlands were hell on horses, and even the tough mustang he rode was labouring in the dry heat. When he dismounted to let the horse walk without his weight, he could feel the heat of the desert floor striking through his boot soles like burning embers.

Twice, he poured water on to his bandanna and bathed the mustang's hoofs and the horse seemed helped by the attention. But he needed the water to pour down the beast's throat, and he used it sparingly.

There was a tank under the sloping rock at Tres Rochas, and the weird sloping slab of stone was hardly a couple of miles south of the trail from Fort Yuma to Gila Bend, but he did not want to be trapped off the trail and in the badlands, so he passed it by after a bit of thought and aimed for the next waterhole which was a good twenty miles away and unreliable at that.

He had set off with two canteens and a water skin slung from the saddle horn, so his need was urgent rather than dire, but the heat seemed to leach the water from his skin even through his clothes.

He leaned from the saddle and picked a white pebble from beside the trail. It was almost too hot to touch, and he tucked it into his pocket and waited for it to cool off, then put it in his mouth and sucked it. The stone made his mouth wet, but the relief was purely temporary.

The Apaches were closer when he topped out on one of the shallow passes along the road. He could see the faint mist of dust even they could not help disturbing back along the trail, and it had halved the distance. Worried, he swung the mustang's head back to the trail and swore bitterly when he saw smoke going up from the rocky ridge ahead. He was trapped.

On the other hand, he thought, as he swept the horizon with his battered field-glasses, there was a notch in the ridge ahead which would take him round the smoke and away from the known trail. At the other side of the ridge, running east to west, was a deep dry wash he had scouted before, and it was just possible he might make his way along it until he was behind the Indians waiting for him at the pass. He could strike north and east again to Gila Bend.

He turned the mustang's head off the trail and headed for the notch at his best possible speed without exhausting the horse.

Five minutes later, he was lying behind a natural barricade of rocks, with the mustang tucked in behind a large boulder, and bullets humming around his ears. The Indians had played him like a fat trout and he had gobbled up the bait and isolated himself off the trail and miles from water.

Night was coming on, and the marksmen out in the rocks were competing with one another as to who would get him and his scalp. His only comforting thought was that they were pouring their lead at his little fortress so fast that they must be in danger of running out. He grinned at himself for even considering it. Any soldier whose best hope was that his enemies would run out of ammunition was a soldier in deep trouble. And he was.

He saw out of the corner of his eye a flicker of movement to his left, and threw a shot at it, which was greeted by a derisive yell, then switched his attention to the right, and was in time to catch another warrior coming out of an apparently empty patch of desert and starting his run towards the rock.

Best chopped him down with a shot which he clearly saw hit the man dead centre, and shot him again before he could fall to the ground. Angry yells greeted the hit, and two more Apaches rose from the ground, ran a few paces, jinking wildly, and vanished again, several yards nearer.

He was pretty certain there were ten of them – nine, now – and he had a rough idea of where they were. This was the third time they had made their jinking runs, and a fourth was due. He put his money and his sights on the position he had last seen the most easterly of the attackers, and got ready to swing his aim.

Promptly two dust-coloured shapes popped up to start their runs, one of them providentially in his sights, and he saw the blood fly when his shot hit the man in the head. He went down like a sack of potatoes, though his companion dived into the ground several yards closer.

At this rate they would be all over him in ten minutes, and he knew he had to move. Trouble was, so did the Apaches, and they began to speed up their charges.

The next one he got totally wrong and was aiming twenty yards too far to the west when the figures appeared and vanished again.

He was carefully working out where the next one would be when it occurred to him he had not looked behind him for several minutes, and he threw himself sideways, rolling to stay below his makeshift parapet just as a knife thumped into the spot where he had been.

He had dropped his rifle, and in any case the warrior was too close, so he rolled again, clawing for his Colt. It came free of the holster just as the Apache bounced up and threw himself at Best with the blade flickering red in the rays of the setting sun. He fell on the muzzle of the pistol and the report was curiously muffled by his body. Blood sprayed, but the warrior who hit the ground was a dead man.

Best rolled away from the corpse and crouched, pistol ready, and his back against the boulders, but no other shadowy figure came from the desert and when he turned back to look over the barricade, there was no sign of the attackers at that side, either.

He was still trying to make out what had happened to the war party when he heard, far to the west, the popping of guns. There was a sharp spatter of fire, followed by a lull and then a measured volley, and a moment later, a second. It was military fire, measured and aimed, and it was the kind of fighting the Apaches relished least.

If his attackers had gone off to join in the attack on an army patrol, they would soon lose their appetite for it. Soldiers taken by surprise do not get time to fire one measured volley, much less two or – a third volley crashed out while he was thinking about it – several.

He could see, in the dusk, horses being ridden away towards the road, and realized the Apaches had heard their ambush plans had failed, and were going off to think about it. Or perhaps his personal ambush band had gone off to join their comrades confronting the army. Either way, he had a chance to get away and he took it, hopping on to the saddle and trotting the mustang over towards the notch he had aimed for in the first place.

He climbed through it, angled back towards the road in the dying light, and by the time it was full dark, was on his way east again, and that much closer to Gila Bend.

By now, the news that the Apache were out and in force had become more important to the army than the despatches which had brought him out in the first place.

When the Spaniards brought their horses into the

American mainland, they knew what they were doing, Best thought as he guided the mustang up the rutted trail into Maricopa Wells.

The horse was as tired as Best, but the sight of the buildings and the smell of other horses brought his head up, and he stepped out more lively over the last mile or so, with hay and water in his mind, and a chance to stand in the shade.

The Wells was a crossroads in southern Arizona Territory, and it looked it: a straggle of buildings and corrals close to the water which gave the little town its name. There was a cluster of wickiups off to one side, where the Pimas scraped out a living from the uncompromising desert, and a sprawling square building which straggled out over the ground, and contained the saloon, the eating-house, the offices of the stage company and a general store which would have graced Tucson itself. There was a hotel for the stage passengers who needed to wait overnight for the next service out, and a small military outpost which also acted as a barracks for travelling military detachments passing through.

Down towards the Pima village where there was a spring, Best could see four wagons drawn up in a box formation. They looked in a sorry state which was not unusual for wagons on the Yuma road. Their owners had walked most way across the Continent and they faced the toughest part of their journey yet.

Their livestock was in a corral next to the wagons, and from the spiral of smoke going up from the centre of the camp, the migrants were sharing their food.

Best turned in the mustang at the livery and ordered him a feed of grain, but he wiped the horse down himself and set the saddle blanket to dry out on the rail near his saddle.

He took the dispatch bag and threw it over his shoulder with his own saddle-bags, then stumped over to the cavalry office to report in, and dropped the dispatches on the sergeant's desk.

'For us?' asked Sergeant Murphy, but Best shook his head.

'Goin' on to McDowell in the morning,' he said tersely. 'I was told to put them in your custody overnight. Here's the chit.'

Murphy scribbled on the receipt and handed it back, then put the bag into the big iron safe behind him.

'There's a bed for you in the bunkhouse. Hotel's full,' he told Best. 'Be in the saloon later? I'll buy you a drink.'

Best winked. 'Don't leave it too late, Murph. Only thing's keeping me awake is my belly's stuck to my backbone. Once I've eaten a cow or two, I'm for the sack.'

The sergeant closed the safe, and took his hat from the peg. It was an old campaign hat which had been bleached almost white by the sun and whatever shape it had been before, it was now a true 'wide-awake' with the front of the brim turned up almost vertically. It was said to be older than its owner, and only the bravest of men enquired if Murphy really was a thousand years old, or only looked it.

He let Best out of the door, and locked it behind

13

him, and the two men walked over to the saloon. It was not until they were sitting by a table in the corner of the saloon, with schooners of beer and shots of whiskey in front of them that Murphy asked the question.

'Rough trip?' he said, trying to make it sound casual and being totally unsuccessful at it. Best nodded, grim-faced.

'Rough as a bear's bum, Murph. Rougher, out beyond Gila Bend. The Apaches are out, and there's trouble at Yuma over the fort there.'

'Run into any yourself?'

Best grimaced. 'Got chased for a while out beyond the Bend. They kept after me to right close in. They wasn't just showing off, neither. They meant it. Trouble brewing for sure out there, and the colonel needs to know. I got to deliver them dispatches, and I got to get back to Fort Yuma right smart.'

The sergeant stared at him for a moment, and saw he was serious.

'Real trouble, you mean? Uprising, maybe?'

'Well, I cut plenty of sign going and coming. Close up to the fort, too. You was scouted plenty last night, and there was a lot of 'em. Stage from Tucson in yet?'

The sergeant nodded. 'Come in an hour back. Changed horses and went on up north. Couple of the passengers stayed on at the hotel, and it picked up a few more before she went. Reckon they're in trouble? Maybe I should tell the captain?'

Best shook his head. 'I'll tell him myself. Need to report the hostiles out on the Yuma road, anyway. Will he be in his quarters?'

The sergeant shook his head. 'He went out on patrol this morning with ten men. I was expecting him back by now, so maybe I should worry.'

Best put down his empty beer schooner.

'So who's in command while he's out?'

'You're lookin' at him,' said Murphy. 'You reckon the captain's in trouble?'

'Not impossible. Which way did he go?'

'Down towards Tucson. The stage driver says he passed the patrol some miles out. Had a quiet run himself. No problem.'

They were interrupted by the arrival of their food, and while Best was sawing a huge slice off his steak, there was a second interruption.

'Excuse me, gents.' A thin man in worn clothes was standing by the table with his hat in his hand. He looked drawn and worried and the sun had tanned him a rawhide face.

'How can I help?' Murphy made no pretence that being interrupted in his dinner was a pleasure.

'I understand this gent just come in over the Yuma trail. That right?'

He was staring at Best as though he hoped it was not right.

Best swallowed and nodded 'Just now. Hour ago, or so. What of it?'

The man pulled out one of the spare chairs at the table and sat without waiting to be asked.

'What's happening, out on the road?' he said. He seemed to be badly worked up over the question, and it sounded anything but casual.

'Who am I talking to?' said Best, without pausing

in his mission to rid the world of half-raw steak.

'Oh, sorry, mister. The name's Wheatley. Ned Wheatley. I'm from Ohio. Me and my family been making for California for months, now, and we reckon to be on the last lap.'

'Well if you want directions, you're on the right road,' said Best. 'Down to Gila Bend, keep west and in time you'll get to Yuma. But I'd leave it a while, were I you. I'm surprised you got this far on your own.'

Wheatley swallowed nervously. 'We didn't,' he admitted. 'We were with a wagon train for most of the way. Big one. Well armed, too.'

Best cocked an eyebrow.

'Where are they now?'

'Man who started us going got us as far as Santa Fe and said he was where he wanted to be, and he stopped there. Left the rest of us to it.'

The story was not unusual: the dissatisfaction with their conditions at home, a failed crop and the prospect of more back breaking labour before the next one came in.

'Mr Babbleton, he said he'd been over the California trail, and he knew it well. Said he'd guide us all there, to the promised land. Then when we got to Santa Fe, it turned out he got land there, and he was all set to settle down. Told us to keep on going west and we'd hit the coast, and that was the last we saw of him.'

'And how much money did he take off you all?' asked the sergeant, in a tired voice.

'Too much. Said he needed it for supplies, and we

trusted him. After all, he was going all the way with us, wasn't he?'

Only he didn't. And neither did their money. Babbleton went off saying he was going to do a deal for their supplies and they never saw him again.

The wagon train broke up. Some elected to go home, a heart breaking journey over thousands of miles they had already covered; some decided to stay in Santa Fe and the New Mexican Territory.

A few, a dozen wagons in all, decided to go on and try to make it through for themselves.

'Then some stayed in Tucson. Two stopped off at the old Mormon settlement along the San Pedro. A few of us came on, and now there's only four of us. We want to push on through.'

Best caught Murphy's eye across the table and pushed his now empty plate away from him. He hated having to talk and eat at the same time, but he could hear the desperation in the man's voice and read it in his eyes. This was not a time for a lesson in manners.

'Well, Mr Wheatley,' he said, picking his words carefully. 'I'm sorry for your bad luck, but if you try pushing on to Yuma right this moment, that bad luck is going to get a whole lot worse. You're heading straight for a whole passel of trouble.

'Trouble is, between here and Yuma, there's a whole lot of Sonoran Desert. That's bad.'

He accepted a thin cigar from Murphy, bit off the end, and lighted it.

'In that there Sonoran Desert, there ain't nothing that doesn't sting or poison or bite. I know you come across plenty of territory that does the same thing, but you got to double it when you are considering the Sonoran.'

The man gestured impatiently. 'We've been through some pretty bad territory just to get here, mister. We know about deserts.'

Best nodded. 'OK,' he said. 'What you ain't come across so far is Apaches. Out there in that desert at this moment, there are Apache Indians whose only goal in life is to come across a cartload of pilgrims with supplies. Apaches love supplies. You might think you ain't got nothing much, but to an Apache Indian, dressed in rabbit skins and lizard leather, you are one walking treasure chest. You got any women with you?'

The pilgrim nodded. 'My wife and daughters, but there's my sons as well. My eldest boy Lucien is a good shot. And I can drop a turkey at two hundred yards.'

'Was the turkey shooting back? Sneaking up on you behind rocks? In company with a group of friends? Your rifle a Winchester with fifteen rounds in the magazine, mister? If it's not, you ain't got enough firepower, and that's a fact.'

Best tapped the ash of the cigar and accepted a cup of coffee from the waitress.

'I seen four wagons out by the Pima camp. Yours one of them?'

Wheatley nodded.

'Maybe if the four of you stick together tightly, and carry plenty of shells, you got a chance. Not much of one, but a little one.'

The migrant looked so depressed that he relented a little.

'Look,' he said, leaning forward on the table, 'you got two choices. You can stay here a while, rest your animals. The ones I saw in your corral looked pretty used up, and they need water and good feed.

'I got to go on up to Fort McDowell tomorrow with dispatches. But I expect to be back within the week and I have to go through to Yuma. You stay here and rest the stock, and when I come back through, we can talk again. If you are all purely set on trying to get through to Yuma, then I can at least go through with you. I know where the waterholes are, and I seen how they are. Maybe if you get in your stores and fill your water barrels, and make sure your stock's up to it, we can get through to Yuma together. How'd that be?'

To his surprise, the man's expression did not change. He still looked worried beyond reason, and he raised his head to say something, when a girl's voice interrupted him.

'Pa?' it said, and all the men in the bar looked up in surprise. The saloon in Maricopa Wells was no place for a woman, and the men all strongly disapproved of women who went into it.

This one, however, was different.

She was tall, slender and her hair was dark as midnight. Her clothes had seen some pretty rough times from the look of them, but her beauty was made greater by contrast. Her eyes were a startling blue, clear and large and at the moment, she was plainly as mad as a rattler with a horse standing on its tail.

'Pa!' she said again and even the hard grained men lining the bar flinched at her tone. 'Pa, you promised Ma there'd be no drinking of strong spirits while we were on the trail! And here I find you in a saloon with glasses on the table in front of you!'

With one sweep of her arm, she cleared the table of glasses, coffee mugs and the remaining cutlery. Coffee sprayed across all three men.

'Just a moment, ma'am!' Murphy protested, wiping down his shirt with a red spotted handkerchief the size of a tablecloth.

'You mind your own business,' she stormed. 'What has this to do with you, soldier boy?'

'Well, you just threw my beer all over the floor, and the coffee I'm wiping off my uniform belongs to this gennelman here – and that's just for starters!' said Murphy, in a voice which had been known to stop stampeding horses in their tracks.

She hardly paused in her tirade.

'And I suppose not one of the glasses on this table belongs to my father? Is that what you are trying to tell me, soldier?'

'Yes, it is,' Murphy roared. 'That is exactly what I'm trying to tell you, me girl! Your father come to us to ask our advice about the Yuma trail, and so far he hasn't had so much as a cup of coffee here! And since you cleared the table of our drinks, neither have we!'

For a moment there, a flicker of indecision passed over her face, but her father at long last got his voice back.

'Emma Wheatley!' he roared. 'You make your

apologies to these here gentlemen, who are being affable enough offer to guide us through to Fort Yuma, and you take yourself out of this saloon this minute! You hear me?'

The effect it had on the girl was dramatic.

'Sure, Pa,' she said, in a voice which had suddenly turned into the cooing of a dove. 'Sorry to have interrupted you, gentlemen. Good night.'

And she swept out of the stunned and silent room like a grand duchess leaving a European court. When she left, she almost got a round of applause.

'Now that,' said a voice from the bar, 'is a woman to cross the prairies with! What's her mother like, mister?'

But Wheatley was in no mood for jokes. He was purple with rage and embarrassment, and he stood up from the table immediately.

'Sorry about that, folks,' he said tersely. 'It seems my little girl needs some manners teaching. Good night, Mr Best, and I apologize for any embarrassment. We'll do like you say and wait for you to come back.'

# CHAPTER TWO

But he didn't, and it cost him dear.

Best came back into Maricopa Wells a few days later, with his errand done and a fort behind him seething like a frypan. The news he brought coincided with growing alarm for the patrol from Maricopa Wells which had still not been heard of since it left for Tucson the previous week.

Best reported the sound of firing he had heard on the road in from Yuma, and instead of receiving an explanation, found he had merely started more alarm. There should not have been a military formation out that way at that time, and the volley fire confounded all the authorities.

He had hurried back to the Wells to prevent the four families from setting off on what now looked like a suicidal road to the west, only to find Wheatley and his family gone.

The three remaining wagons were still where he had left them, and their livestock was still in the corral. The families looked at him with worried eyes when he enquired about the Wheatleys.

'They gone on two days back,' reported Ezra McLennan, the father of the largest family, a grizzled man with four sons who never seemed to be seen without their long rifles, and spoke rarely. All of them were dressed in homespun, and the women were distinguished from the men only by their skirts.

'Hardscrabble' was a word coined to describe the McLennans, and they lived up to every letter of it.

'Sure did,' confirmed the eldest son. He was about to spit tobacco juice into the dust but caught his mother's eye and stopped himself just in time. Mary McLennan had once delivered herself of one of her sons in the middle of a Kiowa raid, and her family swore she never once stopped loading the rifles for her menfolk. She was also a tolerable shot herself, allowed her husband, with a twinkle in his eye, Though these days, she got right testy if there were Kiowas around.

But the McLennans were the only family in the group which had come from the west, and had experienced Indian troubles. The others were from further east and providentially the group had not encountered any hostile Indians on their way.

Mary McLennan deeply disapproved of the Wheatleys' decision to push on without waiting for Best and the rest of the wagons.

'We was all going to be ready to go in a few more days,' she said. 'Movin' on alone when there's Apache devilment goin' on was just plain askin' for trouble.'

Best accepted an invitation to join them all for coffee, and hunkered down on a wagon tongue to drink it. The other two families were very like the McLennans, though they left Ezra and Mary to do the talking. They just gathered round and listened, peering out from under the brim of their hats and nodding silent agreement when Mary trotted out the facts.

'Trouble is, Ted and his folks ain't never had Indian troubles,' opined Ezra. 'Got clear across the country and never saw a single ornery redskin – nary a one! Just cigar store Indians and garrison drunks.'

It was unusual but not unheard of. The spaces were vast, and the Indians of all tribes few on the ground. They were mostly hunters and moved to follow the game, and down on the southern end of the mid-west, with its vast areas of sand and rock, game was hard to find.

If the Wheatleys' first close-up experience of Indians was the friendly Pimas around the Wells, Best could understand that a man without experience might well reason that if these were Indians, he had little to fear.

But the Apaches were not Pimas. Best hoped very sincerely that Wheatley had not yet come across the Apaches, and when he thought about the beauty of the girl he had met in the saloon, his stomach turned over.

He questioned the McLennans carefully and discovered it was need that had forced the Wheatleys out of safety and into the danger of the Sonoran Desert.

'They was broke,' Mary said, topping up his coffee mug with steaming black liquid strong enough to float a horseshoe. 'They took longer'n they planned for, comin' down from Santy-Fe, and their animals was all used up. Longer they stayed here, the less they had to cross the desert, and they was real worried about the malpais.' She used the Spanish word for badlands, Best noticed.

'But they knew about the Apaches,' he protested.

Mary McLennan nodded. 'Said they seen no Indians on their way here, and didn't reckon they'd see any on the rest of the journey.'

She paused and poked unnecessarily at the fire.

'Truth is, I reckon, they stayed here much longer, they'd have eaten up too much of their grub to make it to California. And then there was that girl o' theirs.'

'Emma?'

'Yup. That girl's too danged pretty for her own good. Wasn't a man 'round the Wells wasn't waggin' his tail and howlin' at the moon for her. Her pa was run ragged just makin' sure she wasn't goin' off into the woods with some feller. Soldier boy was the worst!'

She shot him a glance as sharp as a bayonet. 'Didn't take you too long to get back here from McDowell, did it, mister? Gal like that's got men 'round her like bees round a honey pot. All o' my boys was fallin' over their own feet every time she walked past.' She shot a look at her husband, and raised her voice.

'And that includes this moony ol' bull, here!' she spat, and Best grinned when Ezra coloured up under his tan.

25

'Now, Ma!' he protested, and she grinned fiercely.

'Didn't worry me, that girl didn't even know he was alive! But I didn't want her putting ideas in my boys' heads. I started for Californy with five men, and I aim to get there with five men,' she said. Best believed her. She would, too.

But the fact remained that for whatever reason, the Wheatleys had gone off into the desert on their own. He had no option but to go after them and the sooner the better. The McLennans and their friends stared at him as he stood up and finished his coffee.

'What you gonna do?' asked Ezra warily. The boys leaned on their long rifles and watched him hopefully. Best realized that at one word of encouragement, the boys would be packing rations to go with him, and he could not afford any more responsibilities than the Wheatleys. It was going to be hard enough to get them out of danger by himself.

'Tell me about them: how do they travel?' he asked. Prudent travellers moved at night when the heat of the sun was not leaching water from them and their animals, but with the urgency of the trail on them, an ill-advised party might risk day travel as well.

'With us, they done nights only when the heat was off the land,' said Ezra. 'They can't afford to push them oxen too hard. They're pretty used up as it is, and they didn't get enough rest right here when they should have.'

The western trail was littered in its hardest parts with heavy furniture treasured by the family, sometimes over several generations, which was simply too heavy for the draught animals to haul. Stubborn migrants hung on to Grandma's wardrobe and Aunty's mahogany press for too long and some even killed their draught animals rather than abandon family treasures. Their own graves were seldom far from that of their oxen and horses. It was an unforgiving country even for prudent and skilful travellers, and fools died early.

'Them as makes it to the West are the bravest and the strongest,' an old pioneer wagon master had told him once. 'The cowards never started and the weak and foolish never make it.'

He had been helping to bury the corpses of a small group which had been first ravaged by weakness and lack of water, and then fallen victim to Comanches on the trail up from Texas. There were no survivors, and by the time they were discovered, the corpses had been prey for the scavengers. Burying them had not been a pleasant job.

Now, the Wheatleys were out there, and the Apaches were fired up. He filled his canteens and was dipping the water skin in the trough by the spring as he asked his questions.

The Wheatleys had waited only two days for his return, then loaded their wagon and hitched up their animals. They had two draught oxen left from their original team of four, and they had tried hard to yoke their few cattle up to the wagon, but without much success.

They had only one horse which had to double as a draught animal and the hunting mount. The animals could not get both wagon and load up the harder grades, so the family unloaded the heavy luggage at the bottom, hauled the wagon to the top and then hand packed the heavy gear to the top. It could take a whole night of their travelling time and meant progress was agonizingly slow.

Except, he discovered, on this occasion. He followed the road down to Gila Bend, and was told the family had passed through the previous morning. Ted Wheatley had announced that he could be camping on a small island in the middle of the river that night, and it was thought that he had probably made it.

That meant that he might still be there, and would be preparing to move on in the dark hours, so at least he would be well watered and have full barrels. Or if he had moved on, by this time he could be camping at least ten miles on from the river, where there was a long, hard slope for which he would certainly have to unpack his goods.

Best swung back into the saddle and moved on at an increased pace. Once through Gila Bend, the Wheatleys were into the real danger zone, and only crass stupidity or dire need would persuade them to tackle the desert in such bad condition.

But the camp on the island in the middle of the river was empty and the coals were cold when he reached it. He examined the site carefully before he moved on himself, and satisfied himself that this time at least they had survived without incident.

The danger of moving in the daylight was double. The heat of the sun would be punishing to the animals and in the daylight the wagon would be easy to see from far away, and to track from close up.

His face was grim as he hoisted himself back on to the mustang after taking a cigarette break and making himself a pot of coffee. He pulled a strip of jerky from his pack, and chewed on it as he followed the trail out towards the badlands. The sun, risen and savage, sucked the moisture from his body and he watered the horse as often as he could.

He found the bodies at the top of the long gradient he knew was their place of the greatest danger. The wreckage of the wagon was still smouldering on its blackened iron tyres.

Around it were the remains of the Wheatleys' possessions. Their family treasures, those which were of no value to the Indians and no attraction to them either, had either been thrown on to the burning wagon or strewn around the site.

As Best read the sign, the Apaches had caught up with the family when it was spread out on the hill. The children had been gathering up the lighter packages, and carrying them up, and the adults had already taken the heavier packs up to their campsite. The smouldering bones of the family chest could be seen in the blackened wagon bed.

The Indians had come up from the bottom of the slope, and stood with the family around the wagon. What had sparked the massacre, he did not know, but the smaller children had died with their parents around the wagon. Mother and father had been scalped and mutilated, probably after death, but the corpses of the smaller children had simply been left to lie.

Most of the clothing and all of the foodstuffs had been taken, and blankets and tools were missing. All would be of value to the Indians as would the family's small store of firearms and ammunition. Knives had been taken.

He searched carefully among the bodies, and even raked the ashes of the wagon bed in search of some sign of what had happened to the son, Lucien, and the beautiful Emma, but in vain. Both were missing, and his heart sank at the thought of what might be their fate.

There was, of course, a chance that they had managed to hide themselves before the massacre had started, so he circled the site, in increasing circles to try and cut some tracks.

He hit paydirt on his third circuit. The raiders had made their way off into the badlands to the south of the trail and into the mountains. He could see their horses' hoofprints, and followed them into the desert.

They were travelling fast. Their horses were moving along smoothly and it was not long before he picked out the Wheatleys' saddle horse, from its shod hoofs. It was moving in the middle of the group which meant that its prints were often overlaid by those of the animal coming after it.

He had not been travelling long though, when he came across a new set of prints on top of the horses' tracks. They were boots, white men's boots, and they followed the Indians' tracks out into the desert.

Where they had come from he had no way of telling, but the man who had made those tracks was not in good shape. His path wavered from side to side. Twice, he had fallen to his knees and the second time where were a few drops of blood on the ground.

Best found him shortly afterwards. It was Lucien Wheatley, and he was indeed in poor shape. He had wound a strip of his shirt round his head, and clamped his hat on top of it to keep it in place, but there was fresh blood on the shirt. He had no gun, no water bottle, and clutched in his hand as he lay on the ground was a folding Barlow knife with a ground down blade about three inches long.

Best dismounted and turned the boy over. There was more dried blood on his face, and his eyelids flickered as he felt himself being handled, though a half conscious grab for his Barlow knife was too slow and too weak to be a threat,

He responded, though, to water being poured into his mouth and grabbed for the skin, but Best took it away from him.

'Easy,' he said. 'Drink too much and you'll just bring it back up and leave yourself worse off than you was before. Let it soak in. You can have plenty, but slow, or you're a dead man.'

The boy was too weak to put up much of an argument, and he allowed the water to be trickled into his mouth a little at a time. It had its effect dramatically quickly. Within a quarter of an hour he was sitting up and taking sparing sips from a tin cup.

'Feel well enough to tell me what happened?' asked Best, leaving him to the cup, and devoting himself to building a little fire for coffee. The boy – at 16 he was more of a man, really – watched him and began to get impatient.

'Slow down,' Best said, shoving the coffee pot into the edge of the fire and looking out his skillet and a slab of bacon. He fried some thick slices and made camp-fire bread in the fat, then sat back and leaned against his saddle. They were tucked into a small cove overlooking the trail taken by the Apaches, and night was almost upon them. When it got really dark, the fire would have to go because its glow would stand out in the black of the desert like a winking eye.

'Tell me what happened, and where's your sis?'

Lucien was coming out of his shock quickly. At the mention of is sister, he started to stand up, but Best pulled him down again.

'Steady, I told you. I ain't got time to nurse a sick man and track Apaches. I want you walkin' on your own two feet and able to handle a gun. Can you shoot?'

'Of course I can! Been shootin' for the pot since I was eight. But I ain't got no gun. They took them all, them thievin' animals.'

It was a slow process, but Best was patient, and got the whole story out of the boy in the end. The trouble, as he had suspected, was money. The journey first to Santa Fe and then through to Tucson had been much longer and more laborious than Wheatley had expected, and their small store of money was eroded by the delay.

By the time they had worked their way down the

Rio Grande and across into Arizona Territory at Lordsburg, the family was forced to make for the coast as fast as they could.

The pace had been too much for the oxen, and they had died one by one, until only a pair was left. The Wheatleys tried yoking their cattle to the wagon instead, but they were not suited to the task, and did not have the body weight of the draught oxen.

The slower pace contributed to their problems and as the remainder of the wagon train dropped away, the Wheatleys and three other families found themselves on the edge of the hardest part of their journey broke, badly supplied and hungry.

The decision to move on had been taken by the father. He had been trying to persuade himself that the threat of Indians was being exaggerated. They had come across the continent without Indian trouble: why should it strike on their last leg?

But it had. While they were spread out, bringing the wagon supplies up the long hill, the Apaches had come out of the desert.

'One minute they wasn't there. Next they was,' said Lucien. 'Wanted food. They kept rubbin' their bellies and pointin' to their mouths. Pa said no at first, we didn't have enough for us, but they started lookin' in the wagon. He gave them our food for the day to get shut of 'em.'

The Indians had accepted the food, retreated to a distance, sat down and ate it. The Wheatleys began putting the luggage back in the wagon, but the Indians came back. This time they had clubs in their hands, and their manner was more menacing.

Wheatley, worried for his family, reached for his shotgun, but the Apaches struck first.

When he ran for his own gun on the wagon, Lucien was struck down from behind. The last thing he heard was his mother screaming, and the cries of his little sisters.

When he came to, he was lying behind a rock just off the trail. He could hear the wagon burning, and the voices of the Indians as they gathered the horses together. They had butchered one of the oxen and were broiling meat over the fire they had started in the wagon. Lucien lay still.

'Musta passed out,' he said. 'Next time I woke, they was gone. All o' my family was dead, and they took Emma with them.'

Alone, armed only with a pocket knife and a stone, he had set off after his sister's kidnappers. He had no real plan, just the conviction that he was the only man left and it was up to him to do what he could to get her back.

Best sat back and looked at him with new respect.

'How many of them was there?' he asked.

'I counted ten. May have been more, but not too many. Pa always said I had to take my boots off to get past ten,' Lucien admitted.

So the lad had set out after ten Apaches who had massacred his family and kidnapped his sister alone and – though he probably did not realize it – well on his way to dying from thirst.

Men like that built empires, Best thought. For a fleeting moment, he felt a twinge of sympathy for the fleeing Indians.

But at the thought of Emma Wheatley at the mercy of at least ten Apaches, it disappeared.

'Come on, Luce,' he said. 'Let's go find her.'

# CHAPTER THREE

There was not enough light, even with a bright moon, to track at night, and the Apaches could have taken any trail they liked, or none, so though it was difficult to keep the boy in camp, Best handed over his blankets and rolled the boy up next to the embers of the fire, and settled himself under his saddle blanket with his head on his saddle.

Even with his leather coat on, it was cold, and after a while, he got up and threw the saddle blanket over Lucien. The boy moved a little in his sleep, and murmured to himself, but the blow on the head had taken a toll, and he stayed unconscious. Sleep was the best medicine he could have at this time, so the scout left him to slumber.

He himself took his rifle, pulled up his collar and did a short patrol of the little cove in the moonlight. It was deeply cut into the slope of the northern foot of the mountains, and the moon turned it into a study in black and silver.

There was a spike of rock on one of the outer edges of the cove and he climbed up its uphill side until he could see the desert landscape around him.

To the south, the mountain ranges marched away towards the border with Mexico in dramatic black and silver, a huddle of spikes and valleys. Across the silvered landscape, nothing moved. The Indians who had captured Emma Wheatley were well hidden, wherever they had chosen for their night stop.

There was no tell-tale spark of a fire to be seen against the black. No smudge of smoke rose into the crystal clear sky and not a sound broke the mountain peace. He might as well have been on the surface of the moon.

And yet there was life and busy life as well in this eerie landscape. The creatures of the dark were abroad, ranging the ruts and canyons which were their hunting grounds.

All he had to do was wait, and the night would reveal itself to him.

Very slowly, it did so. First the far away creatures emerged from the black and silver. A coyote trotted busily along the trail below, stopping now and again to raise its head and listen and snuff the air. It could probably, Best knew, smell both him and the horse. What tiny wind the night allowed to whisper over the land carried a river of scents on it, rich and pungent to the wild noses out there.

The coyote confirmed his judgement by stopping suddenly. It raised its head, and looked straight at him, and he heard it snarl from where he was. Then, in an instant, it was gone. A tiny puff of dust where it had been was the only clue it had ever trotted along the trail.

He heard a small rustle closer by, and moved his hand from the face of the rock in time to see a small scorpion like a twisted crucifix, walk past, close to his face. Instinctively, he drew back. The little bark scorpions had the nastiest sting, and didn't hesitate to use it.

A rattlesnake left a curious twisted trail in the dust of the approach path to the campsite, but showed no signs of wanting to investigate the remains of the fire within the cove.

Then, just on the fringe of hearing, came the one sound which did not belong in this wild, beautiful landscape. The tiny scrape of a twig on woven fabric, unique and as out of place as a splash of blood on a wedding dress.

It came from the approach ramp to the cove, where some mesquite provided the only skeletal cover in the landscape. And while he listened, it came again. There was something – and since it was wearing clothes, that meant someone – on the path to their camp.

He had let his hat fall back on his shoulders, so the outline of his head and shoulders was distorted and probably not recognizable from down on the ramp. He eased himself behind the rock, and stepped with infinite care down from his perch, and on to the edge of the cove just above the clump of mesquite.

Even from directly above the ramp, he could not see any sign of the stalker. He did not dare use his gun, because where there was one Indian there easily might be more, and even if the enemy were alone – and friends do not steal upon a man's campsite in the dark of night – a shot would be heard miles away.

He was about to move his point of view when the man below moved and betrayed his position. From Best's point of view, it was as though a mesquite stalk came to life and moved silently towards the camp.

For a second the moon picked out the glitter of a knife blade and the warrior, bending low, began to stalk towards the camp. He was totally silent, placing his feet with eerie care, and it was like watching a deadly shadow descend on the sleeping lad who lay there.

The mustang, picketed nearby, tossed his head and blew uneasily through his nostrils. Either his more acute hearing had picked up some sound, or the scent of the Apache had spooked him, for the horse suddenly moved his position, and whickered.

The boy woke up and called out, 'Mister Best? That you?' and the Apache suddenly rushed the camp, still silent but twice as deadly.

Best drew and threw his knife with the same motion. While it was still on its way, he grabbed for his gun, and dropped from the spur of rock into the camp.

The knife, thrown with all his strength, was a clean miss – until the Apache heard the scrape of Best's boots on the rock, and stopped in his charge. The knife and the Indian coincided with an audible thud, and Best's pistol, slashing sideways, caught the man on the back of his head.

The pistol had not been necessary. The heavy, ten-inch blade had gone in under the Apache's raised knife arm and buried itself between his ribs. The breath went out of the Indian in a long, slow sigh, and he fell first to his knees and then face forward on to the ground.

The boy was frozen in the act of rising, and he could not take his eyes off the dead warrior. Best could hear his breath coming in ragged short gasps, and stepped forward to shake him. The last thing he needed was a young man in shock.

But he had misjudged the lad. He was not in shock – not at the appearance of the Indian, anyway. He was staring at the corpse, then went to his knees and started tearing at the vest the Apache was wearing.

Best leaned down and caught his arm.

'He's dead!' he told Lucien in a soft voice. 'Can't hurt you now. Leave him!'

The lad tore his arm away and completed what he had been trying to do. He peeled the waistcoat off the body, and threw it on the ground next to the Indian.

'My Pa's vest!' he explained to Best. 'Thievin' Injun stole his clothes, even! My Pa went to Sunday meetin's in that vest. Got no right . . . no right at all.'

Best realized the lad was fighting against tears, and understood. It was not the garment which upset him, but the evidence that this was indeed one of the Apaches who had murdered his father and mother and all but one of his family.

'Well, you can take it back now, if you have a mind to,' he said. 'Indians always loot clothes. I seen bucks wearin' women's dresses, underclothes, the whole shebang.'

He hunkered down and unclasped the dead

Indian's hand from the knife.

'You got to understand. These people live one jump away from death from their birth to the grave. They could die for any reason. Warfare – they fight among theirselves all the time, and was doing long afore the white man come.

'They can starve in one bad winter. Death from thirst is one bad waterhole away. They can die of cold, even out here in the desert. They got quite good medicine for dealin' with what they generally used to get afore white folks come out here, then we come along, and we brung a whole passel of sickness with us.'

The boy stared at him. 'We did?'

'Sure. I come across some men so mean they'll give the Indians blankets infected with smallpox. Bad enough for whites, but at least we know how to deal with it. Deadly to the Indians. Wipes out whole villages, men women and young 'uns. Spreads like a prairie fire, too.'

The boy gave him a long look. 'If you are tryin' to make me sorry for these murderin' devils, then you are wastin' your breath, mister.

'We was just passin' through, mister. Me and my Ma and my Pa, and the girls. We wasn't stealin' their land, or huntin' their game, or givin' them so much as a cold in the nose. They hadn't got no call to murder my folks and steal my sister.

'We even give them food, food my family needed ourselves to get to California.'

Best leaned back on his heels. The stars and the moon told him night was coming to an end. They needed to get moving.

'I ain't quarrelling with you, friend,' he said. 'No matter why the Indians is like they are, they're still pure poison to you and me. You can understand 'em all you like, but hanging head down over a slow fire will hurt you just as much.

'No, boy. I'm just tellin' you why they're like they are. They're still your enemies, and you still have to be ready for 'em.'

He gestured at the dead Apache. 'Now, I thought I was ready for anything, but this sidewinder still damn near caught me by surprise. The thing to remember about Apaches is that they will catch you every time unless you stay awake for 'em. You just had your first lesson. Now, take this warrior's knife, and keep it sharp. Can you shoot a bow and arrow?'

The boy shook his head.

'Right, we'll find his and learn from it. You can always make a bow and arrows if you know the right plants to get the makings from. More men killed by arrows than bullets round these parts.'

There was also the question of the Indian's mount. Their need for a horse was desperate, and unless this man had abandoned his a long way away, they had a good chance of finding it. They packed up their simple camp and started out in the grey of the dawn with the boy riding and Best leading him and looking for the tracks of the Apache.

The horse was half a mile away, tethered in a pile of rocks which concealed it from the trail. It was an Indian pony, with a blanket thrown over its back and a hackamore bridle tied round its lower jaw.

'Think you can ride him?' Best asked the boy, who nodded.

'Ain't nothin' I can't ride, mister,' he said, and proved it by hopping astride the pony and sticking to his back during a short period of bucking. Best was glad to see he was right, and climbed aboard the mustang with a more relaxed mind.

First thing he would like to do was find out where the Apache had come from, why he was alone and how he had found them.

He followed the tracks of the Indian pony for a while along the base of the valley, but all too soon they turned aside where the Apache had come down from the hills to the south, and the ground became too stony to take tracks.

He cast around for a while, but it was pretty well useless, and he was turning away down to the valley again when a flash of light from halfway up the next hillside caught his eye.

Carefully, he avoided looking at it, or drawing it to the boy's attention. But when they came down from the slope, he said quietly, 'Keep looking at me while I talk to you, but get ready to run. There's somethin' goin' on here, and I don't know what it is. I reckon we're bein' watched, and out here, it can only be Indians. If I yell take off like your tail was afire!'

The lad stiffened but repressed the urge to look around, and nodded.

'Whatever you say, mister. Reckon they're Apaches?'

'There's a dozen names for the Indians in this here desert, but they're mostly Apaches no matter what you want to call them. At least until you can make sure otherwise!'

He chirruped the horse into a trot, and led the way round a buttress of rock standing out from the mountainside. When they were out of sight of the watchers on the far slope he reined in.

'If they're the bunch that have your sister, they'll be jumpy. We try to track 'em down, they're like to kill her and run for it, or double back on themselves and try to lift our hair.

'That sneaky bastard we got last night may just have been a scout who smelled our smoke, or he could be someone they left behind to see if they was bein' followed. Either way, you are ridin' an Indian pony. Don't get took alive, no matter what happens.'

The boy didn't blanch, but his jaw took on a solid set. Best grinned. 'Don't get too worried, boy. I ain't proposin' to get took, and if we was, I'd be just as bad off as you.'

He clucked the horse into motion again, and rode on.

# CHAPTER FOUR

They found the Apache campsite by back-tracking the warrior who had attacked them. It was a painful, long-drawn-out and infuriating job because the man, though he did not necessarily think he would be tracked, had used his considerable skill to make sure the job was as difficult as possible.

He used bare rock as often as possible so as to leave no tracks. The unshod pony did not make the marks on rock that a white man's iron-shod mount would do. But Best was aware of the tricks and knew what signs to look for.

Even so, it was as much by pure dumb luck as by his considerable skill that he was able to pick up the man's route. In order to keep the boy interested, Best passed the time by explaining to Lucien what he was doing, and why.

'They know they're being followed, and that means they'll be watching us. That's why that warrior crept up on us last night: he was sent to find us and decided to stop us himself,' he told the boy, as he bent over yet another mark on the face of a bulge of rock, and discovered it had been made by a passing javelina. He could see the double scrape made on the rock by a slipping hoof.

'Javelina,' he explained, as the lad joined him on the rock, and saw the uncomprehending look on his face.

'It's a kind of wild pig,' he said. 'Little and fast moving. Cleft hoof, so it makes two little marks like this.' He outlined the little scratches on the rock.

'Normally they don't make a mark. This 'un slipped just a little. You can pick out the hoofprints on softer ground easy enough.'

He found the prints left by the Indians by casting in wider and wider arcs. First sign was another slip mark, much bigger than the javelina's and without the distinctive double scrape.

'Pony,' he said tersely. 'Recent. Unshod, so it's an Indian one. Not your sister's horse, boy. That one must be shod, and a horseshoe makes a plain mark. We'll look out for it, and then we'll know this is the right bunch got your sis.'

But he was disturbed at the fact that they were not picking up the marks of the shod horse. Whether it slipped or not, the iron shoe should leave a scrape on the bulging rock outcroppings and along the floor of the canyons, and so far they had not seen one.

The Apaches had had the girl in their hands overnight, and what had gone on in the dark hours he hesitated to contemplate. But they had seen no burial site and no blood, so it was unlikely that the Indians had murdered their captive.

But Best should have seen a shod hoofprint, and

he had not. Either the girl was no longer with this group, which probably meant she was dead, or they had disposed of the horse, and she was riding a pony.

He stood up on his saddle and swept the horizon with his field glasses. He could see neither dust nor signs of movement, which meant that if the Apaches were in the area they were at a standstill.

'And that probably means they're lyin' for us,' he told Lucien. 'Ride loose.'

The trail went on through the morning without incident, though. At noon, he reined in and climbed down to give the mustang a rest. Lucien's tough little Indian pony stood patiently while the boy dismounted, and Lucien was pony-wise enough to put the reins round his wrist while he stood on the ground.

They watered the horses from their hats – Lucien's own hat dripped almost as much water on the ground as the horse managed to get down, and Best was forced to fill his own hat over again.

'There's a seep over west of here,' he told the boy. 'We'll make for it. We can water the horses, fill the bottles and check if the Apaches have been there. I don't know of any other water within reach, but that doesn't mean there ain't any. Indians probably know of others.'

It also meant that if this were really the only water, the Indians would know their pursuers were bound to come there eventually. It was worth their while to ambush the waterhole and simply wait for the trackers to turn up.

He hoped fervently that the Apaches would be too

desert wise to poison the water, which was a possibility.

An hour later he was looking down into the contaminated water of the seep. There was a dead pony lying half in and half out of the water, its throat slit and a broken cannon bone testifying to the reason it had been sacrificed. There was no need for the Apaches to ambush the site. By their act, they considered they had either condemned their pursuers to death or forced them to break off the pursuit and return to the last water source.

Best leaned his arms on the saddle horn and felt the water skin. It was around half full, and he had not yet broached the two canteens he carried.

On the other hand, he had two humans and two horses to water and, at the moment, water was more important to them than anything else.

He could get back – easily – to the Gila. But the time it would take him could take the Apaches down into Mexico and far beyond his reach. He was perfectly prepared to pursue them across the border, but even the US Cavalry would be after him if he did. The Mexican-Arizona border was a very tender and recent scar to the Mexican authorities, and their border patrols were notorious for their rough and instant justice. Besides, Best was employed by the US Army and the officers in charge at Yuma, Huachuca and Tucson would be livid if he got the Mexican Government in an uproar.

He dismounted from the horse, and handed the reins to Lucien while he scouted the waterhole carefully. Sure enough, the Apaches had been there, watered their horses and then spoiled the water by slaughtering their injured animal into it. The dead horse had been disembowelled, and some meat had been cut from its rump.

Lucien wound the reins of both horses round his wrist and joined him on the ground.

'Why did they cut the horse up so?' he asked. 'No need for that, is there?'

Best explained. The horse was crippled and useless as a mount. On the other hand, it was edible food, and its intestines formed a natural water carrier. He pointed where the contents had been squeezed out on to the ground, and the gut drained and washed out.

With the great gut knotted at one end, it made a long, evil smelling water carrier. Lucien nodded thoughtfully as it was explained.

'They ain't heard from their scout since he left yesterday, so he's dead,' Best said. 'We're on their tail, so he didn't manage to kill before he died. That means we're good and we ain't gonna give up.

'So they poisoned the waterhole, took some of the meat from the dead horse and his gut filled with water. How far ahead they are now is anybody's guess. One thing bothers me, though: I ain't seen the prints of a small foot among them tracks, so I ain't sure if your sis is with 'em no more.'

Lucien stared at him for a moment.

'You mean she's dead? They killed her?'

Best postponed his answer while he checked out the waterhole area. Then, 'I don't think so. If they had they'd ha' left her lying. No reason to hide her away and it would have likely stopped us followin' them.'

'What, then?'

'Well I ain't seen no tracks from a shod horse, neither. Unlikely they'd kill that. They would keep it, if only to eat it. So your sister and your horse both disappeared at once.'

The boy fiddled with his reins for a moment and then said, 'So where is she?'

'I reckon they sold her,' said Best. 'If we backtrack to their night camp, I reckon we'll find another set of tracks. And those tracks will lead us to your sis.'

It was a much quicker journey back to the campsite. Without the need to look for tracks, Best was able to cut corners, and they were back there within an hour and a half.

With the knowledge of what he was looking for and where, he soon picked up the tracks of the shod horse, which went east over the mountain ridge and followed a canyon down towards the flats.

It was in company with a half-dozen other horses, all unshod, plus two which were pulling travois which were heavy laden. The scrape marks of the travois went deep into the dirt and, at one point, a leg of one had broken off and had to be balanced up. A set of footprints followed the travois, which meant there were women with the group. None of the women was wearing boots, so the girl must be still riding the horse. The hoofprints of that animal were easy to read.

The senior wives in the little group would certainly not like the idea of a white captive riding while they walked, so there was some reason why her tracks were not to be seen.

'Your sis wear boots?' he asked the boy, struck by a sudden thought. Lucien shook his head.

'They wore out,' he said. 'Pa bought us all some moccasins at Gila Bend. The Indians there were making them, and he swapped for them. Mine didn't fit, so I kept my boots. All the rest wore them round camp, though they was hard to walk in, so they put their boots on for the trail. Maybe Em had her moccasins on.'

So simple that he had not thought to ask about it before. Best went back to the trail and examined the footprints where the sand was soft enough to take a print. Sure enough, one pair of feet left a different track.

'She's still with this lot,' he told Lucien. 'I been worried about the fact we seen no sign of her so far, but here she is.'

Lucien bent over the tracks, and stared at them. Then he straightened up and scratched his head.

'I see the tracks but how can you tell one of 'em from the others?' he asked. 'They all look alike to me!'

Best dropped to one knee next to him and pointed with a twig.

'Indians wear moccasins all their lives,' he said. 'They ain't got a high arch to their foot like white men, and on soft ground like this it shows. This here's your sis. See how there there's an arch in the side of her foot? In soft shoes like a moccasin it shows.'

The boy nodded, eyes intent.

'Apaches and other desert Indians wear high leg moccasins, to protect their legs from thorns and scratches. Keep an eye on an Apache if he starts fiddling with his moccasin tops. They put small items in them and roll them over to hold them. Some keep a little knife in there. Or they slip one down the leg of the boot.'

The boy sat down suddenly on the ground and put his head in his hands. It was the first time Best had seen him show any sign of the strain he must be under, and the scout was surprised.

'Buck up, boy,' he said, a little roughly. 'We'll find her!'

Lucien raised his head, and stared at him.

'I never thought we wouldn't,' he said. 'But I keep tryin' to memorize all them things you keep telling me about tracking and reading sign, and the more I learn it seems to me the more I forget.'

Best gave a sharp bark of laughter, relieved and curiously reassured by the boy's own confidence that they would find his sister. 'You'll do, boy,' he said. 'You'll do fine to ride the trail with.'

He was still uneasy about the boy's reactions when he realized his sister would almost certainly have been abused by her captors during her captivity.

Even women from their own tribe had a hard life among the desert Indians. There was little in the way of comfort for them, and their diet was spiked with creatures and plants no white man would dream of eating, and many would consider disgusting. But the Indians stayed alive where white men would die within days, and it was their traditional food which kept them that way. Best himself had stayed alive in one long spell down in Mexico by watching some Indian women gathering worms off plants on a dry river-bed. They stuffed their mouths with them as they harvested the field and strung the last of the wriggling bodies on string around their necks.

Best had come across a field of similar worms later and, driven by hunger, had eaten them himself. They kept him alive and did not taste as bad as he had expected. But he had watched diners at Delmonico's in Tucson eat snails with gusto, and he had himself tasted shellfish with relish.

'Nobody who examined an oyster carefully ever went on to eat it,' an English lord had told him over a camp-fire up near New River. 'But in the clubs in London, they'll pay a week's rent for a plate!'

Best grinned at him, but remembered that he later did examine an oyster from close up, and decided that short of starvation, the oyster could have its shell to itself.

He was still smiling at the memory when he saw, far ahead and high on the side of the canyon, a tiny rivulet of dust slip down the side of a rock, and just had time to kick his horse into action and cannon into Lucien's mount setting it rearing and bucking.

The shot raised a spray of rocky splinters from the canyon floor and shrieked off in a noisy ricochet. Then their horses were racing, belly down, for the mouth of the canyon, and there was a volley of shots to go with them.

They had found the Apaches after all.

# CHAPTER FIVE

Best pushed the boy on in front as he turned to look over his shoulder. The shooting from the terraces at the top of the canyon wall might be spirited, but at this distance on a dropping shot, it was chancy to say the least.

He could see the nearer misses following him along the floor of the canyon, but they seemed wild shooting. He spurred the mustang again and caught up with the boy as he swung his mount around the end of the canyon wall, and out of sight of the shooters on the rim.

The popping of shots went on for a few seconds but petered out as the marksmen lost sight of their targets. Best took the chance to change direction and travel east along lower foothills of the range, climbing and falling as he passed over its folds.

They had been travelling for half an hour when he caught the sickly whiff of corruption on the wind and the mustang snuffed the air and shuddered uneasily. Its ears pricked up, and its step became tighter and more nervous. He heard Lucien making soothing noises to his pony, and realized it, too, could smell death on the air.

He kept the mustang on a short rein as they came around the buttress of the next bluff, and felt the tremor in its flanks. A slight deviation in the desert wind brought him once more a strong whiff of corruption, and he rose up in his stirrups to look around.

There were a couple of turkey buzzards pecking at something on the ground up ahead and several dark mounds spotted among the scattered rocks along the mountain's foot. A larger mound closer by suddenly became a dead horse with two buzzards pecking at the already sadly depleted carcass. Further away, scavengers with four legs skulked away from him, snarling.

The first of the bodies was still wearing its breeches, torn and ragged. A little further away another sprawled face down behind a rock. From the carrion birds still pulling and tearing at the various bodies, there must be a dozen corpses at least, and he could see the remains of dark blue cloth here and there.

They had found the missing army patrol – though what exactly it was doing so far off course and miles west of where it should have been, he could not even guess.

The boy took the sight of the bodies surprisingly well. His jaw muscles corded the closer he got to them, but he examined each one carefully. There was not much to see. It must have been days since Best had heard the rifle fire far away, and in this desert, meat did not lie long.

He did not bother searching the corpses. Whatever had been there was long gone, and there was no point in scrabbling around in the remains to find some identification. With Indians around, he had no intention of hanging around himself to bury the corpses, either.

Lucien finished looking at the bodies and rejoined him. He had managed to calm the Indian pony, and both horses were quiet enough, a little distance away upwind from the carnage.

'Army?' the boy asked, unnecessarily. Best nodded. The ring of corpses could hardly have been anything else.

'The army's missing a patrol went out just before I come across you and your family the first time,' he said. 'These bodies must be about the right number. I heard shootin' just as I was coming in. Got me out of trouble with a bunch of Apaches been chasin' me up from Yuma.'

'Didn't you check to see if they was all right?' asked the boy.

'Check what? I was pinned down atop a ridge down the road a-ways. The Apaches was distracted by somethin', and went off, and I run for Gila Bent lickety-spit. I heard what I thought was shootin', but I didn't know who was doin' it.

'I reported it to the fort soon as I got in and they said they was sending out search parties. They got a patrol overdue.'

He took off his hat and scratched his head.

'Dunno if they'll ever find 'em down here, though.

They was way off course, and out of line. We have to report them to the fort as soon as we get back. They ain't goin' anyplace, so there's no hurry.'

While he talked, he was watching the skyline for signs of movement, and now he was rewarded with the sight of dust on the shoulder of the bluff.

He climbed back into his saddle, pulled his field-glasses from the saddle-bag and focused them on the skyline.

'Cavalry comin',' he reported. 'I was wrong about the search parties. They must've had some report. We better wait here and I can report what we found.'

The cavalry, when it came plodding up on dust-covered horses, was not delighted with what had been found. The patrol was led by a very junior lieu-tenant who was wearing a regulation kepi among troopers who were wisely shaded by battered campaign hats almost the colour of the desert through constant coating in desert dust.

They came to a standstill and the lieutenant stood in his stirrups and looked round the scene with an expression of rigid disapproval.

'Good day, Lieutenant,' said Best. 'Looks like you found your lost patrol, here.'

The officer gave him an icy stare. 'And who might you be?' he said curtly.

The sergeant moved his horse up into line and saluted as though he were on parade at West Point.

'Pardon me, Lieutenant,' he said, in tones so formal it made Best's eyebrows lift. 'If I may intro-duce John Best, who is a scout attached to General

Crook's command?'

The lieutenant nodded curtly. 'Proceed!' Which left the sergeant with nothing to say, since he already had introduced Best.

'Er . . . well, this is John Best, the scout attached to General Crook's command,' he said. 'Best, this is Lieutenant Carey, recently arrived here from West Point.'

The combination of his attitude and the formality of the introduction told Best volumes about the relationship between the NCO and the officer. He had been dealing with fresh-faced new West Pointers for years since the War Between the States, and recognized a situation stuffed full of problems as a hive full of tetchy hornets.

'Pleased to meet you, Lieutenant,' he said, easily. 'Sorry it has to be under sad circumstances.'

There was no change in the man's expression. 'It is a soldier's duty to face death at the hands of the enemy with fortitude,' he said harshly. 'Make your report.'

Mildly surprised, Best told him what had transpired, and how they came to the site of the massacre. The only change of expression was when the lieutenant heard about the second group of Indians to whom they suspected the kidnapped girl had been sold.

'Murdering savages!' he snapped. 'We will pursue them and teach them what it means to lay hands on a white woman!'

'Er . . . no, Lieutenant,' Best said gently. 'T'warn't them as kidnapped her. It was the Apaches. The

Pimas just bought her. Could be they bought her to save her from more hard usage, and deliver her back to freedom.'

There was no change in the frozen expression. Best was not even certain Carey had heard him. Instead the officer rose in his stirrups again, looked around the corpses strewn on the ground and gestured at the sergeant.

'O'Mahoney!' he said loudly. 'We cannot transport these dead men back to the fort at this time. Give the orders to roll them in blankets and bury them. We can send back from the fort to bring them in and bury them in the military cemetery in due time.'

Best coughed uneasily. There were Apache almost within hearing distance, and he would have been much happier to get the whole party on its way than make the useless gesture of burying the remains – they could hardly have been called corpses – lying out on the desert. They would be dried out within a day or so, and if the commanding officer wanted to make the gesture of bringing them in to the fort, he would know it required more men than the lieutenant had under his command.

He caught O'Mahoney's eye and joined him as he supervised the digging of a mass grave. The officer rode off a little way and started surveying the terrain through binoculars. He was looking the wrong way.

'Does he realize there's Apaches almost within earshot, Pat?' he asked the sergeant quietly.

'There might be,' said the sergeant without looking at him. He paused to roar at the diggers to hurry up.

'Might be? There are! We was shot up coming down from the mountains only a few miles back. Was hightailin' it down this way when we come across these here bodies and stopped to check 'em over. If them Apaches followed us down—'

'They haven't,' growled O'Mahoney. He shot a look at Best under his eyebrows, and the scout realized suddenly that the sergeant was embarrassed.

'What happened, Pat?'

The sergeant spat on the rocks nearby.

'That wasn't no Apaches, Best. That was us! General Purposes up there had us open fire on you and this bunch of shavetails didn't have the common sense to go deaf at the right time.'

Best stared at him, thunderstruck. 'You mean, it was deliberate? He ordered you to shoot at us? Dear God, Pat, that boy lost his entire family less than forty-eight hours back. Father, mother, sisters, baby brother, wiped out in one go. Only reason he ain't dead hisself is he fell behind some rocks and they forgot him in the dark.'

The sergeant stared at him, miserably. 'You mean, he's the only survivor of the Wheatley party? I thought they was taking a break at Gila Bend or back there at Maricopa with the other pilgrims.'

'They run short o' money and grub and decided to push on to Fort Yuma. Apaches wiped 'em out, except for the boy here, and his big sister. Indians left him and took her with them. We're trying to find her now before she vanishes up country someplace.'

The officer was walking his horse back down the bluff, and the burial detail was just filling in the mass grave. It was, Best reckoned, too shallow to do anything but interest the scavengers, but the ground here was rocks and sand, and the pile of stones the men were putting on the grave might slow down anything but a really big predator like a bear.

'Sergeant! Get the men together, and bring those two civilians along. I want a few explanations when we stop for the night.' The tone was arrogant and uncompromising. Best carefully guarded his tongue and his temper at the same time, and swung back into the saddle.

Lucien, who had been helping the burial detail, looked stricken. He said, in protest, 'But my sister! I have to find my sister! She'll be expecting someone to come for her!'

The officer ignored him and started to turn away. Best said, sharply, 'Can I have a word, Lieutenant?'

'No, sir, you cannot! I am not satisfied with your story. That boy is riding an Indian pony, and I want to know why!'

'That's simple enough,' said Best. 'He took it offen an Indian who don't have no use for it no more, on account of he's dead. I ain't got time for all this nonsense, Lieutenant. We need to find his sister, and we ain't got time to waste, because she's getting further away every minute that passes.

'Now if you won't help, which I would'a thought was more important than buryin' some poor cavalry-men who can't suffer no more, then get out o' my way. I got a live girl to worry about.'

He gestured to Lucien to get on his horse, and was turning away when he heard the double click of a pistol being cocked.

The sergeant shouted, 'No, Lieutenant! You can't shoot the man in the back! He's one of us!'

His last words coincided with the report of the pistol, but Best rolled out of the saddle and on to the ground as the bullet whistled past where his head had been. Lucien cried out in shock, and the sergeant swore.

Best was on his feet at the other side of the mustang, with his own Colt levelled over the saddle. The lieutenant was wrestling with the sergeant, who had apparently grabbed the pistol to prevent a second shot. The two men, still struggling fiercely, rolled off their horses and fell on the ground. The gun failed to go off.

Carey came to his feet almost weeping with rage. The sergeant was enveloping the officer's pistol in his huge hand, engulfing the weapon, and his face a mask of pain. He unfolded his hand, and Best saw that the hammer had fallen, and only the web of flesh between thumb and hand had prevented the hammer from hitting the cartridge.

O'Mahoney pulled back the hammer and disengaged his hand, with a sharply drawn breath as the spike came out of the flesh, leaving a bleeding hole. He pulled a handkerchief from his pocket and bound it round the wound, and Lucien got down from his horse and helped him tie it.

Not one of the soldiers had made a move one way or the other in the fight, but Best kept his eye on them. It was touch and go whether they would side with the officer but one thing was certain: if they did, incredible though he found the concept, if he or Lucien had been killed in the officer's rage, the other would have to be murdered to keep him quiet about the real facts.

He had every respect for the men who came through West Point. With only a tiny minority of exceptions, they were fine soldiers and usually turned out to be fine men, as well. Carey was one of that minority.

Out here in the desert, the truth was what the survivors said was the truth.

He was preparing to climb back on his horse, when Lucien, who had been staring at the bluff behind the burial site, said suddenly, 'Smoke, Mr Best! Smoke goin' up back there!'

He followed the boy's pointing hand and saw the first puffs rising slowly on the desert air. Someone was making smoke talk up there, and smoke talk meant Indians and Indians, down here, had to be Apaches.

'Congratulations, mister,' he spat at Carey. 'You hurt your sergeant, you exposed your command to danger and now you told the Apaches we're here!'

'And he tried to murder you, don't forget,' Lucien prompted.

Best shot the lieutenant a look like a Sharps .50 calibre.

'Forget? I ain't forgetting nothin'. We'll talk about that, later.'

# CHAPTER SIX

Carey focused his field glasses on the butte and stared at it for what seemed an impressively long time.

Then he put the glasses away and looked round at his command. The soldiers stared back at him with set, expressionless faces. Best had seen those expressionless looks before on the faces of enlisted men, and it was about as bad as it could be.

The soldiers did not trust their officer, and it showed.

Out here in territory where even the rocks were hostile, soldiers needed to have faith in their officers' ability to look after them. Sometimes that faith was badly misplaced, as in the case of Custer, a brave and experienced soldier whose arrogance had on one single occasion led him into a mistake which killed his command. But Custer had that about him which made men follow him and trust his judgement. Nobody ever questioned his courage, for one thing.

This command was tiny – a score of men, half of whom were new recruits to the cavalry in the toughest region on earth. They badly needed to believe in their commander to get them out of trouble – but they didn't and it was written all over their faces.

One small incident – any small incident – and these men would stampede, and, stampeding, die.

The sergeant saved the moment. He came to attention with an audible slam of his heels, snapped off a salute which almost ignited his eyebrows, and barked: 'Permission to deploy the men, sir?'

Carey looked at him as though he could not remember who O'Mahoney was, then his face cleared and he said, 'Deploy the men, Sergeant. Prepare to defend the campsite.'

Best thought his capacity to be astonished had been reached, but this order stretched it again.

'The campsite?' he asked O'Mahoney. 'What campsite? We're out in the middle of a stretch of flat desert. There ain't no camp here!'

O'Mahoney seemed to know what he was doing, though. He snapped off another sizzling salute, rounded smartly on his heel, and marched to his horse.

'Patrol, prepare to mount!' he roared. The men automatically turned to their horses and held the reins.

'Mount!' and the men were in their saddles like a set of puppets.

'Forward. Forward – HO!' bellowed O'Mahoney, and waved his gauntleted hand forward, putting the patrol into motion. The officer, who still seemed to be in a state of shock, dropped in at the head of the little column, as though he personally had issued the order, and off they went.

Best and the boy tagged on behind because they had little choice in the matter, and found themselves being led towards the hills to the north, and away from the smoke signals.

Best caught up with O'Mahoney, and dropped in beside him. The officer, riding ahead, gave no sign he had even noticed Best and Lucien. His eyes were fixed on the far ridge, and he was riding as though he was on parade, reins held in the left hand, right hand hanging beside his hip. He was a good horseman, and his horse under the coating of dust was better than the ordinary.

Best suddenly realized that Carey was behaving as though he were on parade at West Point. His spine was straight, his kepi, which must be hellish to wear in the desert sun without a sun flap at the back, was exactly level, the peak down over his eyes. His shoulders remained straight, no matter what the gyrations of the horse.

Almost, in the background, Best thought he could hear a good brass band playing parade music.

He stared at the sergeant and found the man looking back at him through opaque eyes.

'How long has he been like this, Pat?' he said quietly. The sergeant rode on for a few paces before he replied.

' 'Bout a day and a half, now,' he said. 'When we left the fort, four days ago, he had a command of thirty. Now, we're down to twenty three. If there was a mistake to make, he made it.'

Best nodded. He had heard of this kind of thing,

but never seen it before. There were officers – and NCOs and enlisted men, come to that – who simply could not handle the conditions of real conflict.

During their training, nothing showed up. They trained like everybody else, performed like everybody else, were apparently brave like everybody else. But at some point something happened to tip them over the edge into unreality.

The important thing was to stay well away from the sufferers and thank God they were not in command.

Now, he knew he was in trouble. Carey, who had drawn his sword and was riding with it resting against his shoulder as though about to mount a charge, was still legally in charge of the little force until relieved of the responsibility by a senior officer. They were in fact under the orders of a madman.

He took a look behind him at the patrol. The men sat their horses easily enough, heads tilted forward against the sun, as they jogged along. After a while, the sergeant performed one of his curious over formal consultations with the officer, and told them to dismount and march.

Carey glanced at them with a puzzled expression, then got down and walked his own mount. The dust rose from the desert floor, and billowed round their legs, but the men stumped onwards.

Best stumped with them, and Lucien imitated whatever Best did.

It felt, thought Best, as he took another cautious sweep of the land with his field glasses, as though they had been caught in a dream. The thought jerked him out of the semi trance he was falling into.

They were not in a dream, they were in the Sonoran Desert. It was not an empty landscape, it was one filled with danger.

He mounted his horse and climbed up to stand on the saddle while he took another sweep of the land with his glasses. Once he was out of the cloud of dust raised by the men, he could see much more clearly, even though the heat made the country shimmer and dance.

There was dust in the air where they had just come from, which was probably their own. There was other dust out to the west of their trail, too. He looked at it, combed the rest of the landscape and looked back. The dust seemed to be gaining on them.

He gave his eyes a rest for two minutes, and checked again. It was definitely gaining on them.

He dropped into the saddle and cantered up until he was alongside O'Mahoney. The sergeant glanced at him, and shot a look at the officer who was within earshot, and slowed down his mount.

'What?' he said, when he was sure they could not be overheard.

'There's a dust cloud west of us which is getting awful close,' said Best.

'Don't tell him. He'll tell you to go and scout it,' said the sergeant, wearily. 'And if you got any sense, you'll tell him to go hisself if he's that bothered, and then he's goin' to tell me to shoot you, and send a trooper. We lost one already that way, and Triggs back there got that arrow in his shoulder goin' to find out what happened to him.'

'Dead?'

'What do you think? Triggs found the body. Says it weren't pretty, he got an arrow in his shoulder he didn't deserve, and it got the new men all tensed up. They're so tight wound you could play "Dixie" on 'em right now.'

Best glanced at the line of dusty men grimly plodding along.

'You better get them remounted, Pat,' he said quietly. 'We gonna need to run like rabbits any time now. Got anyplace in mind?'

The sergeant shook his head. 'You?'

'Yup. There's a cove in the hills about five mile thataway.' He took his hat off and wiped his forehead. He managed to point out the direction he meant under cover of swabbing his forehead and the inside of his hatband.

O'Mahoney nodded. 'Reckon I know where you mean. Think we can make it?'

'We'll have to go lickety-spit. Ain't got time to save your officer's feelin's. You want to give the orders? I got the boy to look after, but I'll be breathin' right down your neck all the way!'

The sergeant didn't waste any time.

'Patrol!' he roared. 'On the command, ride like your asses was afire! Follow Mr Best and the boy, and I'll bring the rear. We're aimin' for them hills.

'Right? Patrol! At the double – GO!'

Best waved the boy on ahead of him, and watched him take off like a jackrabbit, and he tucked his head down, put the spurs to the mustang and concentrated on the tiny notch he could see through the heat-haze.

70

The day was dying, and the sunlight had already turned orange when they started. Behind him he could hear the hammering of the troopers' mounts giving their best.

Further away, like a half heard bird cry, he heard the 'yip-yip-yip' of the Indians. They had been caught flat footed by the sudden charge, but it was not going to last. He wondered whether they could actually make it to the little natural fortress he had in mind, and if, having made it, these green troops could keep their nerve long enough to defend it.

In the event, there was hardly a breath to spare. Even the green troopers rode like race winners, and with the memory of what they had seen at the ambush site to inspire them, they fairly flew.

The final half-mile was a close run thing. He could hear the high pitched cries of the Indians, the hammering of the horses' hoofs, the occasional report of a weapon from the pursuers. The men were holding their fire like veterans, though each man was riding with his Colt in his hand.

The final approach to the notch in the cliff-side was up a scree slope which shifted beneath the mounts, but they climbed it like monkeys and at the top there was the gap in the cliffs he had been aiming for.

It was a knife-blade gap in the face of the cliff leading into a narrow, twisting tunnel. The tunnel in turn led back until its roof opened into a slender gap, and the lower part of the canyon bellied out into a fair sized hall. Best had taken refuge there on more than one occasion, and there were the traces of old fires back under the overhang, which proved that it was not one of the strangely beautiful 'slot canyons' which could fill with flood water within minutes if the weather broke in the mountains which drained through it.

The weakness of the position so far as Best knew was the single entrance. He had been back into the canyon several times, and could not find any other way out of it, in the strange little passageways and tunnels into which the main canyon divided.

It was possible there could be one, he admitted to himself. Indeed, he could not conceive of such a canyon without one. But he had not been able to find it. To be on the safe side though, he advised O'Mahoney to put a sentry at the back of the main cave, to listen out for enemies in their rear.

The patrol filed into the canyon, and rested their horses in the main body of the cave. It was protected from above by the huge overhang, and the men needed no instructions to get a fire going on one of the old fireplaces, and feed it from the remains of the other fires left by former visitors.

Throughout the process, Lieutenant Carey sat on his horse and watched, sword balanced over his shoulder. O'Mahoney dismounted the troopers, set up a horse line, set sentries and collected the water bags together, The officer watched, and the sergeant went through his elaborate pantomime of consulting his officer at every turn, but in fact ran the whole camp.

Best and the boy left their mounts with the horse

line and went back to the entrance to the canyon. There was a natural breastwork of rocks there, and they dropped to hands and knees before crawling up behind the army sentries at the mouth of the cave. The guard was made up of a couple of the older, more experienced enlisted men, and Best recognized them both.

'Hi, Besty!' said one of them, without turning his head. Best grunted a reply and prostrated himself alongside the soldier, and surveyed the desert outside the canyon with his glasses. There was, as he expected, no sign of Indians.

'Know where they are?' he asked and one of the men pointed silently.

'Left their mounts over behind that lump 'o rock down there, and one man with 'em. Then spread out. There's a damned Apache behind every goddam' pebble out there,' the soldier said, 'Ever' now an' then one of 'em moves to a new place, and you see him scurrying, but you can bet your year's pay you don't see 'em lessen they wants you to, and that was only because there was somethin' else goin' on someplace else they didn't want you to see!'

It was a long speech from a normally silent man, and Best knew it showed the tension he was under. He could hardly blame the trooper. The blue-bellies, as they even called themselves, would go through hell and back if called upon, but they needed to be certain their officers knew what they were doing and were not going to get them killed. This officer looked as though he were a bigger threat than the Apache, and it shook their confidence.

'They die just as dead with a lump o' lead in their bellies, Tank,' he said quietly. He saw a flicker of movement away to his right, and shot a glance to his left in time to see a dust-coloured figure erupt from an apparently featureless flat stretch of desert and dart forwards. The warrior was unlucky enough to come up smack in front of his rifle, and he fired without thinking about it, and saw the running figure cartwheel into a cloud of dust.

There was a chorus of angry yells as he did it, and two more warriors performed the same trick at the same time. The two troopers fired as one, and missed, and their efforts were greeted with derisory whoops from the Apaches.

But the sun was pretty well on the horizon now and within minutes it had gone altogether. The desert twilight was short and dramatic, and dark came soon afterwards.

'Keep an eye,' he told the sentries. 'And don't go outside the entrance, no matter what.' Tancred, the elder of the two, spat a stream of tobacco juice over the low parapet and into the dust.

'Aw, that's a right shame, Besty,' he said laconically. 'I was lookin' forward to creepin' around in the desert with twenty Apaches!'

His colleague sniggered. 'What you want, Tank, is to find out if any o' them Apaches is a squaw, ain't it? Got him a real curiosity 'bout them Injun gals, has Tank!'

Tancred shot him a disgusted look. He had been detailed to escort some captive Indian families back to the San Carlos reservation some time before, and

74

they had led him a merry dance on the way. He had lost two whole families, and kept the remaining thirteen only by roping them together by the wrists and untying them to allow them to eat.

At some time during the journey, the missing women and children had rejoined the group in the night and it had been a whole morning before he realized he was back to his original number again. The women had apparently crept off to be with their menfolk, and he had not noticed their return. The rest of the escort was just as flummoxed as Tancred, but for some reason the story had become part of his personal legend, and it had stuck.

Best explained the story to the boy on their way back to the fire, and was rewarded with the first good, honest laugh he had got out of the lad so far. It gave him heart.

# CHAPTER SEVEN

Best did not even notice the boy was gone until he had returned to the fire and looked around for him to share supper. The troopers were still cowed by the presence of an officer they knew was not right in his head, and simply shrugged when he asked after Lucien.

Irritated at first that the lad was not taking rest and food when he so desperately needed it, he first called for him, then wrapped his beef and beans in a wad of camp-fire bread, put down his plate and got up to go and look for him.

There was plenty of scope for the boy to lose himself down in the depths of the hole. He checked the entrance tunnel, the horse lines where the tired mounts hung their heads and chomped on their fodder, and finally, he took a burning brand from the fire and swung it until it flared, and held it above his head as he went down the narrowing passage to the tangle of tunnels at the back of the stables.

The sentry who had been set there was missing, presumably having returned to the fire for his rations, and Best cursed the mad officer and overworked sergeant who had not replaced him.

The boy's track was simple to follow. It led straight back to the first tunnel and disappeared into it. Best swore to himself, but he had no option but to follow where the footprints led.

He was a little puzzled that they should be so confident, until he came across a fragment of hot charcoal and realized the lad must have a torch himself.

Lucien had walked down the tunnel as though he were on a wide boulevard. His steps were confident, strong and deliberate. He kept sensibly to the centre of the passageway, staying away from the sides where snakes might be making their night-time way, and stopped from time to time, presumably to listen.

Back here, the canyon was open to the sky, but only along a very narrow crack, which was offset, so that although the freshness of the air betrayed the fact that there was no roof, he could not see the night stars up there in the blackness.

On the other hand a careful watcher would certainly see the glow of the burning torches progressing along the depths, and note that people were moving down there. It was quite possible that the roof at some point opened enough to let an agile warrior eel through the gap and drop into the passageway to come up behind the camp.

If so, Lucien would be directly in his path, and Best drew his Colt and walked carefully with the pistol cocked in is hand.

His own torch was burning down, and it began to gutter, so he doused it and carried the remaining end in his hand. When his eyes accustomed themselves to the darkness, he found the passage was dimly lit from above, and realized the roof was open enough to let in the moonlight somewhere up there.

By bending close to the floor he was able to make out Lucien's footprints, still striding out confidently, and he began to wonder whether the lad had been affected worse than he thought by the dreadful events of his family's death and his own wound.

He rounded a bend in the narrow passageway, and saw ahead of him on the floor, the silver blue radiance of the moonlight falling on the sand floor. The roof here was either much wider, or the course of the canyon must have wavered until it was in direct line with the moonlight.

He was about to step forward when just on the edge of hearing he picked up a faint sound of cloth rubbing on stone.

Best dropped to his haunches and waddled into the deeper shadow at the wall of the canyon. He sniffed deeply but could not smell any odour of snakes, which partially reassured him. On the other hand, some snakes did not release any scent, said the awkward little voice at the back of his mind. He told it to shut up, and made his way along the wall.

He was almost at the corner where the moonlight was flooding down into the darkness when there was a movement in the dark ahead of him.

He raised the pistol in front of him, then a strong, young hand placed itself firmly over the hammer and action.

Best instinctively snatched back the gun and Lucien's voice whispered almost in his ear, 'Indians! Keep shut!'

Astonished and secretly pleased that the boy could ambush him in the dark, he stood up and, from his new position, he could hear the occasional grunted word coming from close by. Some trick of the night air brought a sudden smell of woodsmoke, and every now and again, he heard a horse move.

It did not sound like warriors sneaking up the tunnel to attack an unsuspecting cavalry patrol, but somewhere around the bend, there were Indians all right, and that meant they were too close from any point of view.

He patted the boy's hand, and stepped cannily up to the bend to peer round it. The sound of the Indians was much clearer, now. He could hear the horses move and the warriors murmuring to one another.

'How many?' breathed Lucien in his ear.

He found the boy's hand and pressed five fingers into the palm. Not the whole party which had chased the cavalry patrol, he knew, but perhaps a part of it. He needed to get closer, and he let down the hammer of the Colt carefully, not allowing the mechanical clicks to become audible, and sheathed the weapon.

Instead, he slipped his Bowie knife into his hand, and carried it low, ready to thrust. With the boy safely behind him, he eased forward with his free hand questing ahead.

Another buttress in the wall, and another corner, and suddenly the firelight turned from a warm glow into a pattern of leaping flames reflected against the far wall. The smell of broiling meat filled his nostrils.

With infinite care, he placed his feet as delicately as a nervous mule deer, and ghosted his way to the corner. There was a blade of rock running from the floor of the passageway out of sight above, but it did not quite touch the opposing wall. He realized that from the opposite side, it must look like the end wall of the canyon. There was a scree slope at the foot of the rock wall just where it did not quite touch the side wall, probably the remains of what had at one time been a complete rocky curtain across the cleft. Through the gap he could see the reflection of the Indians' camp fire flames reflected from the far wall. It made an eerie pattern.

He leaned forward as far as he could and found himself looking through a narrow gap, bounded on one side by the wall of the cleft and on the other by the remains of the curtain of rock. The firelight disappeared if he moved his head to one side or the other, and he realized that the gap was in fact a deep crack, and that he was looking along it from the wide end to a slender gap at the other.

For a moment he was puzzled that the warriors did not know about the crack, then realized that he may be able to see it from what was clearly its wide end, and was looking along the crevice to the narrow end.

He risked a climb up the slope, setting his feet delicately and flinching back from the slightest instability in the rock underfoot, until he could see through the gap.

His view was restricted by the depth of the crack, but it got wider as it rose higher and, by propping himself against one side and bracing his foot on the other, he could see through it.

There was the sound of horses eating close by and,

as he steadied himself, one of the ponies shifted its feet, startlingly close, and blew through its nostrils. He could smell the horses on the current of air passing through the cleft, and realized that it was carrying their scent to him rather than the other way round.

The cooking fire was in his direct line of sight, a glowing pyramid with a cone of yellow light at its tip. He could see several skewers leaning on a rock and hanging their contents over the heat. The smell of cooking meat came to him quite strongly. A voice murmured somewhere to his left and another replied from his right.

He could see neither speaker, but heard their movement. An arm reached into view, and selected one of the skewers of meat and took it out of sight. The chunks of meat on the remaining skewers looked like thick steaks of fish, and he realized the warriors were eating steaks of rattlesnake. From the size of the steaks, it had been a big one, and his scalp crept as he realized it might have been caught in the cave.

He did not know any white man who had mastered the Apache language itself, though most of the border Apache groups communicated with one another and their enemies in Border Spanish, which he spoke and understood easily.

One of the unseen warriors dropped into it even as he thought about it, and more than one voice answered. Best reckoned about half-a-dozen men were in the camp, and they had no idea of the passageway through the rock.

'Where did you find them?' one man asked. There was a grunted reply, and one of them gave a sharp bark of laughter. From the staccato conversation, he gathered two of the group had come by some arms, and were willing to sell or barter them. The others were interested, but not fascinated, and the conversation was desultory.

Best assumed the Apaches around the fire were at least part of the group who had pursued the cavalry. Where the rest were he had no idea, but certainly the whole party was not the other side of the rock wall. They were probably waiting out the night before attacking the cavalry group at first light. It was a favoured time for them to attack, because sentries who had been wakeful but undisturbed all night were likely to be sleepy and off guard in the grey of dawn.

He was turning back with infinite care when he caught the word 'woman' in the mutter of talk.

Alert, he turned back to the crack, and strained his ears. The warriors were divided over the sale of some woman. The rifles they had received in return, he gathered, were old and worn. The woman had been young and promised much enjoyment, argued one man.

His stomach turned at the thought of the kind of enjoyment the Indians had in mind. Apaches' treatment of women prisoners was notoriously brutal, possibly because their own women had been brutalized by successive invaders, starting with the Spanish, who had earned the undying hatred of all the Indians of the South-west with their brutality. The Apache was a good hater – the very word *Apache* was said to mean *enemy* in their own language – and returned brutality to the invaders' women with interest. By contrast they could, if they took a fancy to a child, be remarkably tolerant, at least by their own lights. Captured children, both male and female, were sometimes adopted into the tribe, though the older ones had a hard time of it adapting to the harsh realities of tribal life.

His hearing was inhibited by the narrow crack and the muttered remarks, but he gathered that the Apaches were regretting their sale of the captured woman, which he was almost certain was the missing Emma Wheatley. The warriors were discussing a way to follow the Indian to whom she had been sold, and steal her back.

The one thing which did surprise him was that none of them mentioned the cavalry soldiers who were camping so close to them, and the conviction was growing in him that this was, contrary to his earlier assumption, a different group of Indians from the one which had attacked the patrol.

If so, they might not be aware of the other Indians and the cavalry so close by.

The boy was tugging at the leg of his jeans, and he got down from his spy point to find out what he wanted.

Lucien was pointing at the top of the cleft where the buttress was furthest away from the side wall. He seemed to feel that he could squeeze himself through the gap and into the next cave, and Best, who was closer to it than Lucien, could see he might well be right.

With feline care he got himself down from the crack, and urged Lucien back up the passageway until he was certain they could talk, at least in whispers, without fear of being overheard by the waiting Indians.

'I could get through there!' Lucien was almost bursting with eagerness to try. He kept pointing at the top of the slot canyon.

'Say you did, what would you do then? I can't get through there to back you up, and believe you me, boy, you do not want to be stuck in a cave with six bored Apaches and a nice, hot cooking fire!'

Lucien was stripping off his shirt, and pulling off his hat. Under the clothes, his body was a startling white compared with the tan on his hands and face, and bruises from his ordeal stood out like black patches on a white sheet.

Best grabbed him by the shoulders. 'Where do you think you're goin', boy? You can't go through that crack on your own! They'd fry you with bacon for breakfast.'

The boy shook his head. 'But she's there! My sister, she's with them in there!'

Best realized that although he, Best, had understood a part of what the Apache were saying, Lucien had no idea. He just thought that the band of Apache might have the girl with them.

He pulled the boy further back up the passage to where he could talk more distinctly without being heard.

'Listen, lad,' he said. 'Reason I'm going along with you is that I want to get your sis back as well. Least we can do. But we ain't gonna help her by getting ourselves hung head down over a slow fire.'

Lucien jerked in his grasp.

'But she may be with this bunch!' he protested.

Best shook his head. 'No, she ain't, but she was. This was the band raided your camp, and likely the ones that killed your folk. They certainly took Emma, but they sold her on to someone else, and now they're wishin' they hadn't.'

The boy looked as though he had been kicked.

'Now hold up there,' Best told him. 'I ain't told you the most important part, yet. This lot was talkin' about following up them Pimas and buying your sis back. If they can't buy her, they're goin' to steal her.'

'So, how does that help? She'll be worse off in their hands than she is now,' the boy protested.

'But they ain't goin' to get her,' Best reassured him. 'Best thing we found out was that these warriors think they can steal her back. So these warriors know – or they think they know, anyways – where she's at now. They can lead us to her!'

Even in the dim light he could see dawning understanding on the boy's face.

'You mean, they go to steal her back and we follow them and steal her offen them?' he said.

'Yup. But what we need now is to find the other end of this here slot canyon, and be waiting for 'em when they come out in the morning!'

Which he reminded himself, could not be far off, now. There was a tinge of grey in the boy's face which meant the moon was losing its grip on the desert and the sun was on its way.

# CHAPTER EIGHT

The camp in the cave was already stirring when Best and the boy got back to the campsite. The troopers were rolling and stowing their blankets. There were two fires going and coffee brewing.

Best eyed the lieutenant warily, but the man seemed oblivious to him, and was concentrating on polishing his sabre and its scabbard. Brightly shiny metal was considered to be a hazard in the desert where the sun could raise sparks of light from as little as a broken flint, and the flash of a polished sabre scabbard would be seen for miles, but the sergeant didn't seem ready to warn the man, and Best could hardly blame him.

He caught O'Mahoney's attention as surreptitiously as he could to avoid alerting Carey, and told the sergeant what they had heard through the crack at the back of the canyon. The sergeant listened attentively, and nodded when Best told him they were planning on tracking the Indians to find the kidnapped girl.

'Easiest way for it, I reckon,' he agreed. 'I can't

help you, though, John. I don't know what this feller's going to do, and it'll be all I can do to get these greenhorns back to the fort without losin' more of 'em.'

Best grinned. 'Getting out o' this cave's goin' to be the kicker,' he advised. 'The Apaches won't have gone home, and if they join up with the lot I'm trackin', we're all going to be in trouble.'

He saddled up their horses and led them to the mouth of the cave, ignoring Lucien's longing looks at the cooking fires, where bacon and beans were sizzling. The lieutenant had stopped polishing his sabre and was staring at them with the look of a man trying to remember something. Best was pretty certain what he was trying to remember was why he did not trust Best and Lucien.

'Climb up and ride,' he told Lucien. 'Don't look back. Don't stop, even if you hear me hit the ground. Just go and keep a-goin'.'

They went over the barricade at the mouth of the canyon like show jumpers in a rodeo, and hit the ground running like race winners. There was a startled yell from somewhere out among the rocks, and two Apache warriors were caught out in the open between rocks and the canyon mouth, apparently in the process of creeping up on an unsuspecting camp.

Behind Best, there was an equally startled shout from the sentries who had been caught as much by surprise as the Indians, but two shots rang out immediately and one of the Apache stalkers spun round and fell on his face. The other, hopping like a jackrabbit, just made it to cover.

Ther was a scatter of shots which would have alerted the second group of Indians if they were still within earshot, and then Best and the boy were round the shoulder of the mountain and out of direct line of sight of the ambushers and the ambushed and running free.

Best let the horses' headlong pace slow to a more relaxed run, and then to a canter, and swung to the eastward, where he expected the second group of Apaches to come down from the mountains.

Out of the canyon, he could make more sense of the ground layout. The narrow slot in which the cavalry had taken refuge was a crack across the end of a steep ridge. The near end, the entrance into which he had led the patrol last night, was on the desert, while the canyon, so narrow it could not be seen from down on the desert floor, cut across the outcrop and must presumably emerge at the far side, apparently looking like a crack which did not go right through.

The Apaches who had camped there overnight, and whose camp Best and the lad had scouted, had left the site by the time they got there, and cautiously penetrated to its depths. There was, for a man who knew what he was looking for, plenty of sign of their camp. The fire had been covered with sand and smoothed out, though the embers were still warm through the cover. There were six hip-holes in the sand near the fire, and the horse smell was strong further back against the end wall.

Best examined it carefully and found the crack through which they had listened to the Apaches almost totally concealed by the uneven surface of the wall of the canyon and the end of the sheet of rock which blocked it off. Pushing himself into the crack as far as he could reach, he managed to see into the far depths, but only silent darkness was there to be seen or heard.

'They been gone an hour or more,' he told Lucien when he got back to the horses. 'Embers was still warm, but you could touch them, and if you tried, you might blow 'em back to life. So they didn't hear the shootin' and they won't be comin' back. They went thataway.'

The tracks were as usual hard to follow, but from their direction, he was pretty certain he knew where they would lead, and by checking on obvious signs, he managed to close the gap between them and the Apaches to what he reckoned was a half hour.

They were heading, as he had expected, for the Big Horn Mountains, to the west of Gila Bend. Even friendly Indians tended to stay wide of the soldiers they called the 'long knives' because of their sabres. The Apaches were not friendly and their preferences included ambush and looting and slow fires, so greenhorn soldiers tended to be trigger happy with all Indians until they learned to distinguish one from the other.

Some never did learn because they were not allowed to live for long enough. And they found one such soldier halfway through the long morning.

They were plodding along in the almost invisible tracks of the departing Apaches when a sickeningly familiar smell filled their nostrils. To Lucien, with his parents' deaths so recent in his memory, the smell was enough to have him reeling off his horse, to throw up behind a rock.

Best dismounted and ground-hitched his horse, then walked to the top of a small bluff. He found the trooper there, staked out on the ground, and stripped of his uniform. His clothing had been taken, but his long johns were intact, except where his body had been abused. He had been blinded and scalped, presumably while he was still alive, and his body mutilated.

'I sure hope he was dead when they did that to him,' Lucien said unexpectedly behind him, making him jump.

'If he'd been dead, they wouldn't have bothered,' Best growled, more savagely than he had intended. The trooper could not have been much more than nineteen years old, and for such a short life to have ended this miserable way made him angry.

'Shall we bury him?' Lucien said uncertainly, and Best shook his head.

'We do that, the next Indians along will see the grave and know there's been a white man here and he's still alive,' he said. 'I'd give us six hours after that, tops.'

'Suppose they don't notice the grave? Any case, won't they know from the horse tracks?' the boy asked.

'One Indian pony and a shod horse? We might be two warriors with a captured mount,' he pointed out. 'But no matter what, they'll notice the grave. Reading a trail's easy as reading a book, to these guys.'

They went on in silence, into the mountains, and as soon as they started to climb, he knew they were in trouble.

The slopes of the mountains were rocky and barren, and spotted with saguaro and thick, stubby mesquite. The tracks led up a narrow runoff wash, and Best was suddenly aware that he was now following three ponies instead of six.

Without raising his head, he dropped back and made great play of rolling and lighting a cigarette while he told Lucien his suspicions.

'We lost three of the Indians,' he said, raising the paper to his face and tapping tobacco from his sack into the trough. Over the top of his own knuckles as he did so, he gave a long, careful look at the surrounding country.

Behind them, leading down to the flat, was a fan shaped sand apron where the occasional flood had spread the water-carried rubbish down from the mountains.

The tracks they had been following led straight across it, leaving clear imprints of six separate ponies. The tracks led up the wash and into the mountains, where the narrowing walls of the arroyo swung in a gentle turn to the right, cutting off the view of the top of the runoff.

The trouble was that from the top of the sand fan, there were the tracks of only three horses, so three had at some point left the trail, and he had not noticed.

Looking back, he could see where they must have done it, on a patch of water-spread gravel and pebbles at the top of the fan.

'Keep your eye on the tops of the side walls,' he told Lucien. 'See anything strange – anything at all, even if it ain't all that strange – sing out, you hear?'

'I hear,' said Lucien, his eyes already searching the tops of the low cliffs without turning his head. Best reflected that only a couple of days ago, this young lad had been attacked and left for dead, seen his sister abducted and his entire family butchered, and he was still prepared to fight Indians like a mountain cat. And he was still handling himself like a tough desert soldier.

When I have a son, I'd do a whole lot worse than a lad like this one, he told himself, and lighted his cigarette with a match flocked on his fingernail. It tasted very good, even on his dry throat.

He spotted the first Apache within the next hundred yards. The warrior was tucked into the side of the arroyo behind a scrubby bush, covered in dust and to the naked eye invisible. Unfortunately for him, he was not invisible to a scurrying lizard which was making straight across the floor of the arroyo until it suddenly flitted away in alarm, moving so fast it left tiny puffs of dust in its wake.

The sudden flicker of movement caught the corner of Best's eye and he eased back the hammer of his Winchester as he slid it out of its saddle boot, and leaned the rifle across his knees with its muzzle apparently accidentally pointing at the scrub.

Lucien saw him cock the weapon and froze.

'Do you see them?' he said, nervously.

'One of 'em. Keep an eye out for the others,' Best told him. He heard the lad swallow hard, then Lucien snapped out, 'Yes, sir!' steadily enough.

A moment later: 'The one you can see. . . .'

'Yo?' said Best. He did not know whether to kill the warrior behind the bush now, or wait until he knew where the others were.

'Is he behind a rock on the rim, up to the right?'

Best laughed theatrically and said, 'Where to the right?'

'Behind the big rock. The real big one.'

Almost exactly opposite the one behind the mesquite. A difficult pair of shots with the one gun.

'Keep behind me,' he said, and shot the warrior behind the bush, simply because the rifle was pointed in his direction. The man on the rim instantly popped into sight, rifle swinging to aim, and Best, caught with his long gun pointing the wrong way, dropped it and pulled his revolver instead, and snapped a shot at the rim.

It missed, but the range was long and the upward direction of the shot made it more awkward. The warrior, after banging off one shot which also missed, though only by a hair, dropped out of sight again. Best and the boy kicked their horses into a gallop, and pulled in closer to the canyon wall to make it impossible for the Apache to take another shot without exposing his upper body and leaning forward.

As they got closer to the bend in the arroyo up ahead, Best handed the rifle to the lad. 'Can you use one of these?' he asked, and cursed himself for the question when the boy said indignantly, 'I been shootin' for the pot since I was knee high to a jack-rabbit, mister! Where I was brung up it was shoot straighter or starve.'

Well, he certainly hadn't starved and he demonstrated why the next time the warrior on the lip popped his head up to take another shot.

Lucien shot him without breaking the gait of the galloping horse, and the Apache came over the top of the boulder and half slid, half fell down to the floor of the arroyo.

Then they were round the elbow of the dry waterway, and still travelling upwards.

Best was desperate to find out what happened to the third Apache who had dropped back apparently to ambush them, but there was no sign of him.

Apache you can't see is more dangerous than the three you can, he told himself and grinned at the memory of the old Indian fighter who told him the saying. The fierce old man killed Indians with the dedication of a rat-catcher, and it had not taken Best long to realize that a rat-catcher was exactly how he thought of himself.

That merciless breed was not dying out so much as being killed off. Sooner or later they found themselves in a corner with no way out and only Apaches on the outside; the wise ones shot themselves rather than be captured.

Best might not be one of them, but he always kept the last bullet in his belt just in case. An Apache with his blood up was not likely to make any distinctions between the former husband of an Apache woman and present enemies.

And he still did not know where the third Apache had gone, or even if the remaining three had continued after the white girl, or were waiting somewhere in ambush.

# CHAPTER NINE

Both the rifles carried by the Apaches were single shot Spencer carbines taken no doubt from some unfortunate ambushed horse soldier. One had been broken across the neck of the butt and mended with a binding of rawhide dipped in water to harden and tighten it. The repair was remarkably firm and the rawhide greasy with sweat and use.

Best smashed it beyond repair and gave the other to Lucien, along with the handful of fat .56 calibre shells both warriors had in their ammunition pouches. The stubby rifle was heavy but it had a good range and a stunning punch. It was lucky that neither of the Apaches had managed a hit. That fat slug would have knocked either Best or the boy out of the saddle and done terrible damage.

Lucien examined the carbine carefully and loaded a round into the action. Then he looked up and smiled. 'Let's go find me a target,' he said.

Somewhere around there was a missing warrior and not too far away another three. The Indians' aim was to get to the girl before anybody else did so, but they had the added asset of knowing where she was likely to be, whereas her brother and Best had no idea, and would have to follow their enemies to find out.

The trail ran on up the mountain heading for a notch in the skyline, which turned out in time to be the entrance to a pass.

The trail of the three Apache horses led on through the notch, though there was no sign of the fourth man, and Best was developing one of his itches between the shoulder blades. At the top of the arroyo, the land flattened out into a saddle over the ridge, and there were only two horses' tracks on the trail. Best began to sweat suddenly. He thought he had worked out what had happened.

Assuming there were two in front and two behind, he and the boy were boxed in. The Indians knew they were there, and being Apaches it was a fair bet they already had plans afoot to deal with their pursuers.

As soon as the thought occurred to him, he swept the reins across the horse's neck and turned abruptly off the trail and along a game track which followed the line of the ridge among the saguaro and the bushes. Broken boulders turned the trail into a twisting, uncertain path, and he could hear the boy following on behind him and having trouble with the pony. Better now than under fire, later.

His tortured pathway twisted and turned among the rocks, occasionally dropping so that he lost sight of the ridge, and then climbing up through the cactus until he thought they would top out and skyline themselves. He knew the terrain around this area, but not in detail, and the path he was following was totally new to him.

It was more than a game trail, so it must lead somewhere, and his only problem was that if it did, then it was probably known to the Apache, and he had no way of knowing whether they were also following it or not.

Among the broken rocks and hard earth of the mountainside, he could see no scrape marks or disturbed undergrowth, and did his best not to leave any sign himself. The Indian pony, when he looked over his shoulder, was following doggedly on behind him, and Lucien was riding comfortably enough, He had devised a couple of straps which acted like stirrups and apparently made his seat more comfortable.

Suddenly, to his amazement, Best could hear the sound of running water. He had never heard of a spring or a creek in this part of the country, though he did know there must be tanks and springs somewhere, because the Indians travelled here without having to carry large water stocks, but he knew little of them.

He stopped the horse, tossed the end of the reins to Lucien, removed his hat and sidled almost on all fours up to the crest of the ridge which was just ahead of him. As he reached it, the sound of water got louder, and he looked over the crest with enormous care to find himself looking down into a sharp cutoff in the rocks and into a little valley.

At the bottom of the valley was a basin into which

a small waterfall dropped, splashing from a rocky outcrop in its fall, to make cool music in the hot air. Beyond it, the mountainside rose again, in steep, rocky slabs and rough hewn steps towards the real crest of the range. Around the basin grass grew in pockets in the rocks, and a small, narrow trail descended from his viewpoint, and climbed the opposite side of the valley to disappear round the shoulder of the mountain beyond.

For a long moment, he stared at the water, then raked the hillside beyond with his eyes, looking for movement. There was none. Simply the incessant music of the water and the occasional cry of a bird, quartering the sky. Turkey buzzards, he thought, scouting for meat in an empty daytime terrain.

He wriggled backwards from the edge, stood up and walked back to Lucien and the horses.

'Little valley over the ridge. We'll water there,' he told Lucien, and mounted his horse to lead the way over the sharp edge and down to the pool.

Lucien greeted the sight of the valley with round eyes and a look of delight. The sound of the water alone made the day seem less baking, and the taste of it was delightful. An overhanging slab of rock kept the pool itself in shade and that in turn kept the water cool. Best took off his hat and watered the horses sparingly from it, before giving in to temptation and plunging his whole head into the pool.

He held it down for a few seconds, then sat upright and stood guard while Lucien did the same. Their water bottles were submerged in the pool to fill up.

They sat back in the shade of the rock and he let the horses drink again, sparingly.

'Where are we?' asked Lucien. He was cleaning the action of the Spencer with a twist of scrap calico from the tail of his own shirt, and getting a surprising amount of dirt out of it.

'That's better,' he said, without waiting for an answer. He worked the action of the carbine again, and it clicked into place without resistance.

'Where are we?' Best drank again from the pool. 'Hanged if I know. I didn't even know this valley existed afore I looked over that there ridge. Ain't been up here as much as I should, but I sure need to get me a look around.'

He peered around the little valley as he spoke. It was almost like a moment frozen in time. Within the little basin nothing moved except the shadow of the turkey buzzard overhead, and the falling water. The horses had managed to find themselves a patch of grass near the pool and were cropping contentedly, their bellies watered and their cinches loosened.

'How'd that Indian pony take to your stirrups?' he asked the boy, and the lad grinned at him.

'We come to an arrangement. He don't snap at my toes and I don't kick him in the mouth,' he said. 'The stirrups stay. Dunno how them savages stay on so well without 'em.'

'Thighs like vices,' Best grinned. 'Don't ever let one get astride you, boy, or they'll break your ribs and backbone both.'

Lucien laughed out loud. It was the first time he had given a genuine guffaw since the massacre, and

Best noticed it and welcomed it. The boy would never get over the fate of his family, but that laugh was a long stride on the way to learning to live with it.

He glanced at the shadow on the rock beside him. It had moved a good foot since they had stopped here, and it was time they got on their way. He had to get out of the tiny valley, up on to the mountain and find out where the Apaches had gone, and the daylight was leaching away faster than he liked.

'Time we was on our way,' he announced, and climbed to his feet. He removed his hat and peered carefully around to make certain the edge of the basin was clear. It was, and he walked over to retrieve his horse.

It was as he bent forward to take the reins in his hand that he suddenly realized the shadow of the buzzard no longer flitted across the basin. Surprised, he stepped back and looked up to locate the bird and, as he did so, there was the report of a rifle and his saddle horn exploded into a cloud of debris in front of his face.

With bits of leather in his eyes, he dropped to the ground, grabbing for his gun. The horse, spooked, reared and ran for the side of the basin, and a flying hoof caught him a glancing blow on the side of his head.

It was dark when he opened his eyes and he could still hear the sound of the water falling into the basin. The desert cold had closed in, and he was shivering, while his head rang like a cathedral bell.

He began to roll over, and the boy's voice said,

'Stay quiet, Mr Best. I ain't sure I got him, yet.'

Best stayed quiet, and tried to control the chattering of his teeth. From where he was lying he could see the loom of the big rock against the stars, hear the water falling into the basin, and even, when he listened carefully, the sound of horses snuffling nearby.

Lucien passed him a canteen and he drank gratefully, rested and drank again. It was cold and pure and tasted good, but his head slammed like a cabin door in a high wind. He examined it carefully, gently probing with his fingertips. The pain was bad, but his head did not feel spongy, and the bleeding from the broken skin had dried.

For a short time Lucien was gone and, when he came back, he announced himself with a low whistle. Best welcomed him back cautiously, gun in hand, and let the hammer down gently only when he was sure the lad was not followed.

'There was only the one, and I nailed him,' Lucien said briefly. 'Score one for my family. The tab ain't paid yet. Not by a long chalk.'

Best understood his feelings, but he was uneasy about the venom in the boy's voice. It was only too easy for people who had lost their families to Indians to think of all Indians as the same, and see them only as targets.

However, crouching under a rock in the dark of night was no time to plant doubts in the boy's mind, so he kept his peace and promised himself to talk to Lucien about it later.

'What happened to the horse?' he asked. Lucien

gave a short bark of laughter and pointed across the pool. Best could see his arm outlined against the water.

'Listen and you'll hear them,' said Lucien. 'Your horse ran as far as the edge of the bowl, then came back. That's how I got the Apache. He was comin' for your scalp, and the horse distracted him. I reckon he thought it was ridden, and someone was comin' for him, too, and he turned round to look and I shot him. Hell of a kick that there Spencer's got, but it nailed him good!'

'They're famous for it,' Best told him drily. 'Ask any cavalryman.'

'Sure has one hell of a kick, though,' opined the boy.

'You should try it from the other end,' said Best. 'It's a killer.'


With the water and the returning consciousness, his head was feeling better. He still felt as though he had been kicked by a horse – which, of course, he had – but he no longer wondered if death might have been preferable.

'You sure that Apache was alone? Certain sure?' he asked. Lucien nodded, and Best realized with a slight shock that he could see the gesture clearly. The moon was moving round and would soon shine into their refuge. They had to go, or they would be picked out like performers in a spotlight.

'Time we was moving,' he said, and got to his feet. His head reeled, and he had to steady himself on the rock, but after a moment, it settled down to a steady pain, and he settled his hat on it carefully.

Lucien disappeared again and reappeared leading the horses. They mounted up and just as the moon started to shine into the valley, they followed the track up the hillside and over the crest. No rifle cracked, no arrow whispered, no triumphant yell greeted their appearance on the crest.

Further on up the mountain, the moonlight silvered the rocks, picking out the crags in black and silver. Nothing moved up there, and the only distraction within sight was an owl, ghosting over the hillside about her nightly business.

Best did not like to travel at night in unknown territory, particularly among broken rocks, where a pool of shadow might hide a leg-breaking fissure in the stone. But they had no choice. The little gulch with the waterfall might have been a welcome refuge for them, but it would also have been a trap if Indians came, and in the heat of the desert, they were bound to come to the water. Best and the boy would not have been able to get out without exposing themselves to attack.

'Can't be lucky all the time, and we're pushin' our luck already,' he explained to the boy, and Lucien nodded seriously in agreement. He made a good pupil, calm and thoughtful.

Together, like ghostly spirits in the desert, they went out on their hunt.

# CHAPTER TEN

There had been six of them when they started out from the San Carlos. Now there were three, and Vittorio, leader of the Apache war party was bitterly conscious that the failure was his.

He had been the one to suggest the sally from the San Carlos reservation. It was a barren and cheerless place, which did not matter quite so much as the lack of opportunities for a young man to prove himself by taking loot and making women weep in the enemy wickiups. He had been the one to provide the rifles and two of the horses. It had been his idea to raid the lone wagon and its white family when the white man was foolish enough to leave the safety of the Bend and head out at night along the river trail to Yuma.

Vittorio was a travelled Apache. He had been raiding down into Mexico when the fancy took him, or along the old Spanish missions when they were populated – and when the defences were in bad repair, as they had been at Tubac – and he had been across the Sonora desert to the west as far as Yuma on a previous occasion, and looked with awe on the great, smoke-belching boats which puffed their way up the Colorado against the current to Fort Yuma and beyond.

He had even, from a safe distance, seen the great stone house the white men had erected on the bluff over the river, and in which the men in curious striped clothing were kept. He understood the concept of a jail, so he had no trouble working out exactly who the men in the jail were and why they were there. His very soul shrivelled at the thought of being locked up in that stone box behind the woven steel bars and never let out.

Better death than the living death of being buried alive in that terrible place, he thought, and made his way back across the desert to the land of his people where the white men were interfering and changing everything he held dear.

And now, after he had brought his young men out on their raid, he had lost half of them. He was ashamed and he was angry, deep within his soul, at the people who had brought about this state of affairs.

The three Apaches crossed the open land north of the Big Horns and stopped at a waterhole in the elbow of the curved range to the north. The Pimas they were following had stopped and watered there before them, and they recognized and identified the horse on which their quarry was riding from the faint tracks, and knew that the group had passed there at least a day and probably more, in front of them.

But they were a large family group. The women were walking, and they had to stop each day to camp.

The Apache warriors, mounted on good horses and now well watered in addition, would catch them up the following day.

Vittorio stood for a long time on the high ground above the waterhole, staring back the way they had come. He knew the two white men were following him, though he did not know where and how they had picked up his tracks, and the uncertainty bothered him. He did not know, either, what had happened to the three warriors who had dropped back to take their scalps. The warriors had disappeared and failed to reappear.

It followed then that they did not return because they could not, and the only thing which would have prevented them was death. Was it possible that the white men following had been skilled enough to ambush and kill them?

There was no dust in the air along their back trail, which meant that neither the warriors nor the white men were travelling behind him. The land was dry and the air was still. If there were travellers back there, so there should be dust.

Yet he felt uneasy.

The trail ahead was clear enough for him. The Pimas were travelling slowly and seemed to be heading towards the mountains to the north-east. There was a blue-coat soldier army post there, and the Pimas would be able to camp under the shadow of the post.

For the first time it occurred to him that the Pimas might intend to deliver the girl back to her people. It was not unknown, and the white men were known to reward such acts. The soldiers would protect Indians who performed them, too.

He had to catch them before they reached the protection of the post, though this should not be a problem. The quarry was travelling slowly and the warriors quickly.

Yet he hesitated before he jumped down from the rock and rejoined his waiting companions. Either the white men or, more likely, his warriors, should have dealt with their enemies and be following on behind.

Maybe the whites had won, but lost his trail? He dismissed the thought. At least one of them seemed able to follow tracks like an Apache himself. If they had somehow ambushed and killed his warriors, then they should be back there, raising dust.

His two remaining warriors looked at one another when he came down from the rock and gestured northwards. The missing three Apaches were on their minds, too. Where three had gone, three more might follow.

Being Apaches, they were not afraid, of course. Not of anything human and tangible, at any rate. But was there not something other-worldly about the invisible pursuers who had swallowed their companions and yet raised no dust, gave no indication of whether they were still on the trail or not?

It was an uneasy trio who headed northwards for the river. And not one of them looked to their north and eastwards, over the flat land between them and the white man's settlements at Vulture where men delved in the ground.

There was dust there, momentarily, but without a wind to move it, the dust merely fell back lazily to the ground. And where it fell, a practised and expert tracker would have found the tracks of one shod horse and an Indian pony.

To their north and east Best, on the other hand, was looking in exactly the right direction, because he had planned to overtake the Indians by taking to the level ground between the Big Horns and the water-hole, and moving fast careless of his dust.

They had managed to overnight at the Vulture mine, managed to re-equip themselves, and at the same time pick up a crumb of knowledge which was invaluable.

They had been told about a group of Indians trav-elling with a white girl and making for Fort Whipple.

The news had come from an unexpected source as they were leaving the mining settlement at Vulture. As they rode out of the gateway arch, a blanket-wrapped figure on a paint pony was coming in. It was an Indian, and he was, the sentry said as he turned him away, as drunk as a skunk and smelled twice as bad.

Best glanced at the Indian and was greeted with a stream of broken English, and an extended hand.

'What's he want?' asked Lucien, who was careful to keep his eye on the blanket-wrapped figure and his carbine pointing the same way.

'Don't worry, he's a Pima,' Best said, and was pick-ing up his reins to steer round him when the Indian came out with another babble of words. Best stopped, and stared at him.

'What's up?' asked Lucien.

'Says he's got information about a white woman to sell if I give him a drink,' explained Best.

'Reckon he might have?' The Indian picked up the enthusiasm in the boy's voice and turned his attention to Lucien. To emphasize his point he leaned closer and grabbed at the boy's sleeve.

Best knocked his hand away, and shot a few sharp words at the Indian. The man's face took on a grotesquely exaggerated look of deep cunning and waved his hand in refusal.

'Says he'll tell you, not me. Wants a bottle of whiskey. Givin' whiskey to Indians is an offence, and any local army officer will lock you up for it. They can't take strong drink. Look at him now, and he's probably only had the local version of tiswin.'

'What's that?'

'Hooch they brew from some kind o' cactus. They use it for a religious ceremony mainly, I guess, but to guys like this buck, it's poison.'

Lucien could see that. More important, he could smell it. But the Pima had mentioned seeing a white woman, and there was only one white woman he knew about up here.

He grabbed Best's arm. 'Can't we give him some beer or somethin'? If he saw a white woman, that's gotta be her! Can't be two of 'em, can there?'

Best knew perfectly well that there could be several white women in the hands of Indians in Arizona and probably were, but he agreed with the boy that such an obvious lead could not be ignored.

110

On the other hand, the miners at Vulture were always having to defend themselves against Indians, some of whom were perfectly friendly when sober, but hell on wheels when drunk.

'You got a bottle round here?' he asked the guard, but the man shook his head.

'No I ain't and if I had I wouldn't give it to you, even if that drunken blanket-head had the secret of Montezuma's gold ready to sell. I know this guy. He's only halfway there at this moment, but give him a couple more drinks, and he'll try to scalp the entire Eighth Cavalry, startin' with me!'

'You in the Eighth?'

'Nope. That wouldn't stop him, though.'

Best was calculating how long it would take him to get back to the saloon and buy a fifth of rye when Lucien solved the problem himself. Desperate for information about his sister, he swung the carbine towards the Indian, pulled back the hammer and shouted, 'To hell with him! If he won't tell us where my sister's at, he's no use to me! I'll shoot the bastard's head clean off right here!'

Whatever the sentry and Best thought of the threat, the Indian certainly took it seriously. He suddenly straightened up on his pony, and made to jerk at the bridle. Best stopped him just in time before he galloped off into the desert, and the man suddenly gabbled out a string of perfectly understandable English.

'Go Fort Whipple!' he shouted. 'Indians look for reward from horse soldier chief! Buy her, take her Whipple!'

Best let go of the bridle and the pony was off like a racing greyhound, its drunken owner swaying crazily on its back with arms waving like a palm tree in a high wind.

'There, you got your answer,' the sentry said triumphantly. 'An' no need to give a Indian firewater. Don't you ever try that round me, mister. Out here, Indians and whiskey don't mix – not ever!'

Lucien was already trying to turn the pony. 'Which way's Whipple?' he asked. 'Just point me that way. That's my sister we're talkin' about, and she's out between here and the fort with a bunch of Apaches after her. Which way?'

'North, a tad east,' Best told him, pointing. 'Whipple's yonder, but—'

He was talking at the back of the Lucien's head, for the boy was already whipping up the startled pony in a headlong run for the river, which was many miles away. The guard watched him go, with a mock admiring grin.

'Whoo-eeee! Lookit him go!' he exclaimed, admiringly. 'How far you reckon that pony's goin' to go before he founders? Ten, twelve miles? More?'

Best groaned and kicked his own horse into motion. The Indian pony might be a tryer, but the big mustang had the legs of him and he quickly caught up with Lucien and grabbed at his rein.

'Where do you think you're goin' in such an all-fired hurry?' he said patiently as the boy's horse came to a stop.

'Whipple, o'course! My sister's—'

'Your sister is somewhere between here and the

112

mountains up yonder, with a bunch of Pimas. They won't be goin' fast because their women and children are with them and they won't be mounted. Neither will your sister by this time. Indians believe warriors ride and women walk. The Apaches are all mounted and by my calculations, they'll all, Pima and Apache, have watered by now, just south of the mountains, there.'

'And then?'

'Then they'll be heading for Prescott and the fort there. Looky there!'

The boy followed his pointing arm and saw, low against the mountains top the south, a faint haze.

It was dust and dust meant travellers and travellers, here, meant either the Apaches or the Pimas. A wise man would turn right around and go back to Vulture.

They headed instead for the mountain to their north, to head off the Apaches who would steal the girl yet again, and this time Best did not even like to think about what might happen to her if they succeeded.

# CHAPTER ELEVEN

If the dust he could see was caused by the Apaches they were hunting, they must be making very good time, Best told himself for the third time as they changed their direction yet again to catch the dust cloud they were trying to intercept.

When they had first seen the faint traces of dust in the air, it had been well to their south, near the mountains. The dust was not constant, of course. It appeared and disappeared according to the terrain the horses were crossing. Deep sand, and dry dust and up went the dust; hard rock and stone and it vanished again.

But he had observed it where it should have been when they first caught sight of it, and were tipped off by the drunken Indian as to where the Pimas were taking their captive. Now, it was a good deal further north, and if it kept on moving at that speed, he would have to change their heading yet again.

He had no reason to believe it was not the Indians they were trying to head off. An Indian, he had worked out, could cover forty miles a day easily, and nearly fifty if he was prepared to kill his horse. Even on foot they could cover phenomenal distances, and fight like cats at the end of it.

But this bunch was really travelling. He noticed another mist of dust further north than it should have been, and swore venomously.

'What's up?' said Lucien.

'I been real stupid, that's what's up!' Best told him disgustedly. 'I been watchin' the wrong damn dust!'

'Huh?' the boy looked puzzled.

'That dust cloud up there' – he pointed to the northerly one he had been watching – 'that one's a different bunch from that one.' He pointed further south, where a second and much smaller cloud could now be seen against the loom of the far off mountains.

Lucien swung in the saddle and checked them out, then swore himself.

'And there's another bunch over there,' he said, pointing.

So there was. Best dug out his field glasses, and stared at the foot of each of the clouds. There was movement at the foot of each which indicated horsemen. On the most northerly, the one that Lucien had just pointed out, the picture was even more confusing.

Three lots of people were converging on the surface of a wide valley normally empty of human activity, and he and Lucien, at the moment raising no dust at all, made up a fourth.

He pushed the field-glasses back into his saddle-bag and shook out the reins.

' 'Bout time we raised some dust our own selves,' he said, and kicked the horse into action.

Far ahead of them, Emma Wheatley plodded through the heat and dust, following the mule which had until recently been her mount. She had been unceremoniously tipped off it as soon as the Apaches had sold her to the Pimas, and the animal was now towing a pair of long poles made into a loose hammock by the addition of a few cross-pieces and a pile of blankets.

On it were several packages of blankets and some hides neatly stacked, containing smaller packages, most of which smelled. In this heat everything smelled: the horses smelled, the blankets and the hides which were used to cover the wickiups at night smelled.

She had come across the concept of a wickiup only after coming into the south western territories. Until then, she had thought all Indians lived in tepees. She had seen plenty of those on her journey across the country, and could understand the usefulness of a tall pole-and-pelt tent to a people who followed the migrations of the game which formed their staple diet.

A wickiup was, she realized, merely a tepee with its sticks bent over to make a domed frame. The frame was laced with twigs and branches and covered with skins to keep out the weather. It worked like a tepee, in a country where getting long, strong poles was almost impossible.

She had learned quickly not to argue with the

Indians, men or women. Men simply slapped her face – and they slapped hard – and from their outraged expressions she gathered that being contradicted was not tolerated. The women were similarly intolerant of any rebellion, but more helpful. Once it had been established that she was not allowed to argue, they would generally demonstrate what she was required to do, and even help her do it.

The walk through the desert was no trial to her. She had been walking all the way across the country since her father had decided to make for what he called 'The Promised Land' in California. Just why he thought people in the west would be more tolerant of his religious fervour than they had been further east, she did not know, but he seemed certain.

A shadow flickered across her face and she glanced up, to see a turkey buzzard plane across the sky between her and the sun. Close up, she found the birds unlovely and even disgusting, but she could not help taking pleasure in their grace and mastery of the air, as they rode the hot updraughts of the desert with their pinions twitching like feathered fingers to control their flight.

When she had been little, she had flown kites with the children from neighbouring homes, and she knew how to catch the hot air and make the kite soar, and how easy it was to lose it, and have the graceful flight turn into a fluttering fall.

A grunt interrupted her reverie, and she started and looked round to see one of the warriors riding near her. For once, he did not scowl and snarl at her,

117

but pointed at the buzzard, linked his hands to emulate the wings, and grunted a word at her. She realized he was naming the bird for her, and imitated his voice as closely as she could. He actually grinned, then, and repeated the word, and this time she got it more or less right. He gave an approving nod, and turned away, scanning the land over their back trail.

Following his gaze, she thought she could see a vague mistiness in the air against the remote mountain range behind them. The warrior stared in that direction, then called out to his fellow scout on the far flank of their advance.

That man, too, stared long and hard to the south, then drew the attention of the other men in that direction.

The group, which was stretched into a straggling line flanked by the menfolk on their ponies, tightened up into a more compact group. Most of the men closed in round them, and two dropped out of the line of march and galloped off in the direction they had come. She remembered that they had passed a rocky outcrop earlier on, but before she had a chance to see if that was where the warriors were heading, she received a smart clip across the back of the head, and one of the older women hurried her back into line.

The whole group was hurrying, now. They deviated their line of march from the direction they had been taking, and headed for a gap in the mountains range ahead and to the right. It was not hard to work out they were making for a known refuge.

She looked questioningly at one of the younger

women who was hurrying along next to her, and the woman saw her enquiry, and grunted, 'Apache!'

Her heart sank, and the memory of her nightmare hours in the hands of the Apaches who had murdered her family rose in her throat like a sickness. Her feet suddenly found themselves hurrying faster than ever.

One of the girls called out what was obviously a comment on her hurry, and the rest of the women laughed. One of the men, bringing up the rear, grunted an angry comment, and faces straightened, and backs bent. They really covered the ground.

They were closing the mountains, and by this time were obviously heading for a particular narrow notch in the range, when one of the scouts came back from the south. He grunted his report to the warriors who were flanking the line of march, and one of them went off at a fast clip obviously to replace him as scout.

They were almost running now. The mounted men, first chivvied the walkers, then began to pick up the children and the old people and take them on their horses. Nobody came near her, though once or twice she saw the man who had spoken to her about the bird glance in her direction.

Their flight was now almost headlong. One of the warriors rode on ahead, disappeared into the notch in the mountains, and shortly afterwards appeared again, waving them onwards.

The scouts came in from the south again, but by this time the whole group were beginning to climb the scree slope to what was now clearly a desperately narrow canyon.

She was pushed ahead by two of the other women, one of whom was carrying two small children, and making heavy weather of it.

On an impulse, she reached over and took one child, a boy, in her arms, and began to run with him for the narrow opening. The woman, at first surprised and a bit apprehensive, let her take the boy and ran with her.

Together, they slipped into the narrow canyon and, to her surprise turned almost immediately sideways and followed the gash in the rocks, which climbed sharply, following the line of the mountain.

Ahead of her, one of the ponies was scrambling up the slope with its pole trailer catching and banging on the rocky path. The woman whose baby she was carrying pushed her hard from behind, helping her scale the slope, but she had no need to chivvy her. Emma would have climbed the sheer side of the canyon with the baby in her teeth rather than fall into the hands of the Apaches again.

The group topped out of the narrow canyon and climbed past a pile of boulders in its throat which seemed precariously balanced. As she passed it, she noticed it was supported on the downhill side by a tangle of smaller boulders which formed a wall and support.

One of the warriors was standing by it with a stout wooden stake in his hand, and he hurried her past the pile and out on to the top of the cliff.

When she topped out, she realized she was in a prepared position, and understood the Indians' hurry to get there.

She was standing on a wide, sprawling ledge of rock, which was overhung by the side of the mountain above. There was a neat, dry-stone wall along the outside edge, coming to breast height, behind which were a number of regular piles of head-sized stones. It did not take a lot of imagination to realize they were meant for bouncing off head-sized heads, should any attacker be foolhardy enough to try climbing the cliff.

Back against the wall of the mountain she could see several fireplaces with the rock above them blackened by the smoke of a succession of fires. They would accommodate quite easily twice the number of people in her group.

At the far end of the ledge was a stone built corral, like a stable without a roof where the horses were already being herded. She was gazing around her in wonder when she got the accustomed cuff at the back of the head, and was pushed towards one of the fireplaces.

She looked over her shoulder to see one of the older women, whom she had christened 'Crow' because of her black hair and hooked nose. She was a cross-grained woman who would rather cuff than talk, and she tried to grab the baby away from Emma.

The baby, who had been snuggling into her shoulder, a warm if smelly bundle, pulled away from Crow and cried out, and his mother immediately came over and took him from her.

Crow snarled at the mother, but clearly decided to take her revenge on Emma and raised her hand threateningly.

But Emma decided she had taken enough. As Crow swung her hand in what was clearly intended to be a resounding slap, she ducked under the blow, and punched her as hard as she could on the nose. Years of holding her own in a schoolyard full of boys went into that punch, and Crow, taken totally by surprise, walked straight into the travelling fist and went down as though she had been clubbed.

Emma immediately turned away from her and squared up to what she confidently expected to be a concerted attack from the other Indians. But she was amazed to find the rest of the Indians simply staring at her.

The girl whose baby she had carried called out some comment, shrill as a bird, and the rest responded with curious grunting noises she suddenly recognized as laughter.

They had accepted her. She was no longer a sullen captive but a fellow fugitive, she had helped bring the children to safety and she had stopped being a victim.

Behind her there was a snuffling noise, and she looked down to see Crow dazedly climbing to her feet. She was holding her nose with one hand, and one of the men this time called out some comment. Emma did not understand it, but she recognized the tone. He was making a joke.

It went down well and even Crow managed a painful grin under her hand. She walked past Emma, keeping a cautious distance, and started to build a fire.

The incident was over, and somehow, subtly, the

attitude of the Indians had changed. Emma went to the mother of the boy she had carried and started to help her unload the travois which was attached to her former mount. The woman nodded at her and pointed where she was to put the packages.

She was accepted into the tribe, for the moment at any rate. Emma suddenly felt good about it.

# CHAPTER TWELVE

Best climbed down from the rock and into his saddle. He and Lucien had been travelling as fast as they could to catch up with the Pima party and its captive, but they had not managed to go fast enough to beat the Apaches.

Now, they found themselves between two parties going in the same direction, the original Apaches they had been trying to outrun and the newcomers, who had cut in from the east and taken up the chase themselves.

'How do we know they're Apaches?' asked Lucien, pointing to the newcomers. In a remarkably short time he had become almost as adept at seeing the faint dust trails as Best himself.

'Because the Pimas are runnin' from them,' Best told him shortly. 'Maybe we can't see them but them Pimas surely can, and they ain't stickin' around for nobody. Yup, them's Apaches, sure as grandma beats the eggs. They're makin' for Hole In The Mountain by my reckonin'. Once they're in there, they're as safe as houses.'

Lucien looked round. The dust from the south was closing on them slowly, and the dust up ahead was still following the Pimas.

'Which way do we go?' he asked.

Best pointed towards the mountains. 'We've come to get that sister o' yours and that's just what I aim to do, Luce,' he said. 'We go up there because that's where she's at. No point goin' no place else.'

Lucien peered dubiously at the converging dust clouds. So far, it was true, he and Best had held their own against the Apaches they had seen, but he was under no illusion. They had been lucky – truly, really lucky. They could not count on luck alone for much longer.

'How we goin' to get up there?' he asked. 'Won't they fight us off?'

Best glanced sidelong at him. 'They might,' he conceded. 'We'll just have to hope we can convince 'em contrarywise.'

He led the way northwards, taking a long swing to the west to get round the approaching and unknown numbers of Apaches from the east, and rode onwards into the hills.

It was a long pull, full of dust and heat and the sun was going down in one of its dramatic swoops for the horizon by the time they were actually approaching the notch in the hills which indicated the narrow canyon. By this time, the two Apache groups were almost upon them, and within a couple of miles of one another.

Above them, against the side of the mountain, they could see the warm glow which indicated that the Pimas, no matter how close their pursuers, were cooking. Best, who knew the terrain, was leading, and he dismounted as they got to the strewn slope which led to the entrance to the gorge.

Lucien stepped down from the pony, and patted its nose fondly, nearly losing a couple of fingers for his pains when the animal snapped at him. He felt the tombstone teeth brush his fingertips, and suppressed a yelp of indignation. Best chuckled in the dusk. 'Treat him rough, and he's likely to do what you want. Show weakness and he's goin' to kill you,' he warned. Lucien scowled but kept his peace.

Best looped the reins over his forearm and hunkered down on his heels. He pulled a couple of strips of dried meat from his saddle-bag and a hunk of bread from their stay at the Vulture mine workings. Lucien accepted both hungrily, and began to tear at the meat with his teeth. The horses, watered from Best's hat, tucked themselves up nose to tail and stood hipshot in the dusk.

'Be full dark in a couple of minutes,' Best said in a low voice. 'Take an hour or so for the moon to come up. Then we move. The Indians generally don't like to attack in the night, so they'll be hunkered down over to the east of us, and them that's been trying' to catch up all day'll likely to the same. They're tied down for the night. But they do believe in attacking with the dawn, when a man's sleepy and don't expect nothing.'

'But if you know that, so do the soldiers,' argued Lucien. 'How come they still get surprised?'

Best chuckled. 'Hanged if I know, son, but they

126

still do. Man seems to get sleepy just before dawn, no matter how long he's been up, no matter how well he knows that's the danger time. And the sentry's the first one they kill, so you'd think he's the one who'd stay awake, no matter what. Just don't work out that way.'

He lay down, using a rock for a headrest.

'Get some rest, Luce,' he said. 'I'll wake you when it's time to move.'

Some chance, thought Lucien to himself as he copied Best and propped his head on a sloping rock. Sleep? On a pile of rocks with the Apaches within a cough and a spit of me? Not a prayer.

Best woke him when the moon was fully up and picking out the rocky slope to the canyon mouth in dramatic contrast. The horses were restive, swapping their weight from one hoof to the other with a muted clatter now and again.

'You ready to move?' Best handed him a canteen and he washed his mouth out with the brackish water and spat it on the ground before taking a long drink. Then he capped it and handed it back, wiping his wet mouth with the back of is hand.

'Sure am,' he said. 'Where we goin'?'

'Up there,' Best said. He was pointing up the apparently sheer face of the cliff to where the dying glow of the Pimas' cooking fires still reflected from the overhanging cliff.

'Fair enough,' said Lucien. 'How?'

Best took up the reins of his horse and swung into the saddle.

'Follow me and I'll show you,' he said, and

grinned at Lucien's silver-and-black mask of incredulity.

He led off through the rocks, the horse's hoofs sounding loud as sledgehammers in the dark. Lucien, on his unshod pony, felt he was almost shuffling by comparison.

They threaded their way through the rocks until he realized with a start that they had entered the shadow of the cliff side, and started up the slope into the canyon mouth. Nothing happened to interrupt them, no yells broke the silence, no leaping figures sprang from the boulders, waving spears and axes.

They entered the canyon mouth, and the horses' hoofs sounded even louder. He was certain by now that they were heading into an ambush which would be sprung at any moment. Best stopped and, nervous as a new-born kitten, Lucien cocked the Springfield. The double click seemed almost deafeningly loud in the darkness.

'Hold your fire,' Best's voice murmured in the dark. Somewhere up ahead of them, a stone rattled and Best called out something in a guttural voice. From up ahead, another answered him, and the horse moved forward, emerging in the end into the reflected moonlight at the top of the canyon.

He could see Best in silhouette riding up to the top of the track, his hands held out sideways and visibly empty, as he guided his horse with his knees. Another flicker of movement in the gloom and then Best called back, 'Come ahead, Luce.'

He urged the pony upwards, and joined Best on the broad ledge. He was surprised to see just how big it was, and at the far end, the horses' heads in the corral were outlined against the moonlight.

A rock near his knee came to life and turned into an Indian warrior carrying a carbine very like his own. The man stared at him with interest and asked something of him in a series of grunts.

'He wants to know if you are Emma's husband,' said Best, gravely and chuckled when Lucien said, 'Hell, no!'

The Indian seemed to understand his indignation if not his words, and gave a sharp bark of laughter. He slapped Lucien's thigh and turned away.

'He says to get down and he'll put the horses in the corral. We will have to make sure we get the same ones back,' said Best. 'This bunch are capable of trying to switch horses on us. Have to make sure we get the right sister, too. Seems this here buck has more than a passin' interest in Emma.'

He gave a short guffaw and swung down, unsaddled his horse, and carried the saddle and his carbine over to the wall, where he dumped it next to an unused fireplace.

'We stay here until we're invited closer in,' he said. 'Sit down. Look tired.'

That part at any rate was not difficult, though Lucien was desperate for a sight of Emma, and said so.

'Listen,' said Best. 'So far as they are concerned, she's their property now, bought and paid for. We can't just ride up and take her away. They got property rights in her so far as they are concerned. They ain't takin' her to Fort Whipple for fun. They want money, or more likely trade goods for her.'

'So we can't rescue her?'

'Sure we can. But not until they've sold her.'

Lucien gave in and rolled himself up in his blankets. The heat had gone out of the desert remarkably quickly, and he said so.

'Lot higher up here than we were down near the Gila,' explained Best. 'We've been climbing all the last few days. Don't sleep too soundly, either. Them Apaches are just waiting for the first grey of dawn, so no matter who else is awake, we'd best be.'

It was nowhere near dawn, though, when Lucien, who was sleeping closest to the end of the ledge, heard the first cautious scrape of sound coming from the narrow canyon, and sat upright, tense and totally awake. He glanced over to the pile of stones ready to block the narrow entrance to the ledge, and then sat upright, and reached over to alert Best. His hand fell on empty blankets.

He was just about to call out when a hand was placed gently on his shoulder, and he closed his mouth. Best's voice, a low hum of sound, was almost in his ear.

'Sentry's missing. Get your gun,' it said.

He already had his hand on his carbine under the blankets, and he eased it out and came to his knees. The fires along the ledge had fallen in on themselves and become piles of gently glowing ashes. The moon was still shining brightly out in the desert, but it had moved a long way since he had lain down in his blankets. The night was nearly over.

He could see Best's outline against the sky, as the scout moved over to the parapet which looked down into the canyon. The man disappeared briefly, and then was back.

'Someone moving down there,' he said. 'I'm going to take a look. Make sure you don't shoot me when I get back. I'll give you an owl hoot. You hear something, no hoot, you shoot. OK?'

Lucien nodded, realized he could not be seen and grunted a reply. Then Best was gone, and he was alone behind the pile of rocks which topped the trail in. So far he had not even seen his sister, though he realized she could only be a few yards from him along the ledge.

Best was more deeply worried than he liked to hint to Lucien. He had also slept lightly by their fire for a while, but awakened when he heard a stone rattle. It had been a long way away, and down the canyon, but there should not be a rattle down there at all. The Apaches might be waiting for the dawn to attack, as was their habit, and since he and Lucien had managed to ride right up to the canyon mouth and up it without provoking an attack, the Apaches out there in the desert were sticking to their traditional pattern.

But there was nothing that said they could not get into position for a dawn raid, and the fact that the sentry was missing bothered him. With their traditional enemies all round, the Pimas should have been more than usually jumpy and alert.

He eased his way down the canyon, sticking to the

131

dark side of it, out of the dying moonlight. The canyon was narrow and by contrast with the waning moon, very dark. He moved down the slope a few yards and stopped to listen. The silence was absolute, when it should not be.

Assuming the sentry had moved down to investigate, he ought to be somewhere around. If he was not around in the lower canyon, the animal life which emerged after dark should be moving.

Yet there was no sound, not even the tiny scurryings of the night dwellers. He hunkered down and unbuckled his spurs, wrapped them in his bandanna and tucked them into his shirt front, reminding himself not to drop flat on his face, whatever the reason.

Then he moved down the canyon a foot at a time, stopping to listen after every few steps.

Silence. An unnatural stillness which signalled danger more loudly than a bugle call.

Best had almost reached the floor of the canyon when he heard the first sound, combined with a wave of a smell compounded of wood-smoke and sweat, and it fastened him to the spot as though he had been nailed down.

The sound was a sharply drawn breath and the faintest whisper of a foot slipping on rock. Best was on his knees with his revolver in his right hand instantly, but even so, the hard-swung knife just parted his hair and left a shallow cut in his head. The blade was sharp and stung like a scorpion, and Best whipped his own knife from his left boot.

He struck upwards, felt the point go home, and his

hand was covered in a rush of hot blood. The Indian fell forward on to the blade and the weight of his body coming down drove the razor sharp steel upwards and inwards. The body that collapsed on to Best was already a corpse when it hit him.

He twisted the blade to avoid getting it trapped in the muscles and pulled it out, shoving the body away from him. As it fell, its own knife clattered on the rocks, and after a second, a low whistle sounded from further down the trail.

He backed up the slope as silently as he could, remembering at the last moment to give a hoot an owl would have been ashamed of, and shouldered Lucien aside as he rounded the pile of stones.

'Apaches!' he shouted hoarsely. 'Coming up the canyon. I got one, others was close behind him. If anyone shows in the gap, drop him!'

He ran along the ledge until he reached the first blanket wrapped bundle which was already sitting up and reaching for an axe.

Best just managed to catch the hand with the axe before it brained him, and bellowed in the warrior's face, 'Apaches! Wake your people!'

He turned back to the cliff top barricade in time to see Lucien rise from behind the pile of stone and swing his carbine butt first into the face of a shadowy figure which was coming round the rock pile. The attacker vanished backwards and a startled yell from further down the canyon alerted the awakening Pimas.

Best arrived at the end of the rock shelf as Apaches boiled through the narrow entrance. Lucien shot the first one in the chest, and Best, drawing his pistol, fired steadily into the entrance gap. He could not see beyond the darkness, but he reckoned he was making the gap – and the narrow canyon neck beyond – into a very unpopular place for running Indians.

A shot banged in the darkness beyond the gap, and Best saw the muzzle flame light up another warrior in silhouette and aimed at it. The hammer fell on an empty chamber, and he was knocked aside as a man came from behind him yelling on a high note, and buried his axe in the head of another Apache.

Abruptly, there was a silence. He could hear the women shouting angrily behind him and risked a glance over his shoulder. Two of the Pima men were down, one with an arrow sticking out of his ribs and another with blood running, black in the faint light, down the side of his head.

Best crawled to the gap and risked a look through. He could just see the ramp which led to the shelf entrance, but it was empty. Lucien who had come through the whole thing miraculously without a scratch, was methodically reloading his rifle. There was another carbine, broken at the neck of the butt, lying by his foot, and the corpse of an Indian stretched out on the shelf just inside the entrance.

'Watch out for that one,' he advised Lucien. 'They'll risk hell, damnation and Methodism to get their dead back.'

'They can go join him if they want to,' Lucien told him with a grin and waving the cartridges in his hand. 'I got me plenty of tickets on that stage right here!'

'They'll be back,' Best told him and, as though they had heard him, the Apache were back, bursting out of the canyon entrance like a plague of demons, pushing back the defenders by sheer weight of numbers.

Best fired, levered the Winchester, and fired again and again. He could feel the barrel getting hot in his hand as he worked the loading mechanism, and the rifle jumped and thumped into his shoulder.

When it fell silent, and the hammer fell with a click instead of a report, he reversed it and swung it like a club. Once, twice, three times, and each time missed the head he was aiming at.

Finally, he swung the rifle with one hand and triggered the Colt with the other.

And then it was over. There were two more corpses lying on the shelf of rock, just inside the rock barrier, and three blood spots just on the ledge, and nothing else.

Best stepped over the two corpses, and looked cautiously down into the gorge. In the growing light, he could see that the approach ramp was empty. There were two discarded lances down there, both broken, and he could see an axe lying further down alongside another big blood spot, but not a single live Apache was in sight.

They had gone.

# CHAPTER THIRTEEN

So were the sentry and the white girl they had come to rescue. As the dawn light grew, and the Pimas counted up the cost of their dawn battle, it became obvious there was no sign of their white captive or of the man who was supposed to guard her and them.

The women who had been wives to the dead had started their mourning wailing and were throwing ashes from the fires over themselves, while the warriors scouted the canyon for signs of their pursuers. Best had to sit down with the leader of the group and persuade him to tell them what had happened.

The Indian was not inclined to answer questions, but when he heard that Lucien was the girl's brother, he grudgingly consented to talk about it.

Yes, he had bought the girl from a group of Apaches who had captured her from a wagon train. He was genuinely surprised to find that the 'wagon train' had been just one wagon, but not to find that the Apaches had murdered the whole family apart from Emma and Lucien.

'They are fierce people and without pity,' he said, as though it explained everything. He did not quite shrug, but the gesture was not very far away. He seemed – and probably was – more upset about the reward he would now not be receiving from the soldiers at Whipple than about the fate of the girl.

He was not surprised to find his sentry was missing along with her, though his eyes darkened and his voice hardened when he spoke of the danger to which the man has exposed the rest of the group.

'She filled his eye. He could think of nothing else but her. I am not surprised he took her away, but I am surprised that he left his people in danger. When I see him again we will speak of this, and then I will kill him,' he said.

He dusted his hands to show their talk was over, but Best produced a plug of tobacco and the Indian accepted a bite off the end, and sat chewing for a while with evident pleasure.

'He has taken her so that he will not have to give her up at the fort,' he conceded eventually. 'But they do not have horses. The Apache will follow them. You bring the Apache to us!'

Best was talking as much with his hands as his mouth. He spread his hands out, palms down in a gesture of denial. 'I followed them to you. We know that the Apache sold the girl to you. We know that they mean to steal her back. She is our flesh, our blood. Can we let this happen? You know what will happen to her if the Apaches get her.'

The Indian stared at the fire for a moment. One of the women was heating a knife blade to cauterize her

137

husband's wound, which was long and deep, though
Best knew that, wound and all, he would be up and
walking as soon as she had finished. The recovery
rate of Indian medicine was higher than the army
medical corps, with one or two notable exceptions.

Eventually the man spoke.

'If a person tell you where to find the girl, then
you will take her back to the fort?'

'Yes,' said Best. 'Me and her brother, who is here.'

'So there will be no payment for Pimas who have
saved her!'

Best glanced over at Lucien. 'He's worried they'll
get no reward if they hand her over to us. May know
where she is, but he isn't letting on for the sake of
saving his money.'

Lucien stared at the chief. 'He know she's my
sister?'

Best nodded. 'Sure does. Just wants his reward.'

Lucien chewed his lip. 'How much he goin' to
lose?'

Best asked. The Indian's eye took on a calculating
gleam, and he spoke at length. Best turned to Lucien
with a twisted grin.

'Roughly the equivalent of the purchase price of
the White House accordin' to this guy. I reckon he's
going to settle for a couple of horses and some blankets in the end. Maybe some cartridges if he can steal
them easy. Though the army won't like that or
condone it. We'll have to find him some our own
selves.'

He turned back to the Indian and a period of furi-
ous bargaining involving much hand gesture ensued.

Twice Best lost his temper and stood up, making angry signs which even Lucien could understand, though both times he sat down again, and more gesturing and grunting ensued. Eventually, he stood up for the third time and stepped back.

'We need half-a-dozen blankets, a pound of tobacco, needles, and a couple of good, sharp knives. I've also promised him a small keg of gunpowder and a lump of lead. They got some flint-locks they can use, and they cast their own bullets for those.'

'How in the name of Joseph and Mary we goin' to get all them goods?' Lucien was amazed that Best had promised so many things they would plainly have difficulty obtaining.

'Worry about that when we get to the fort. I got a few favours I can call in, up at Whipple. We'll manage even if I have to steal. That girl's more important than anything.'

He turned back to the Indians. There was an exchange of hand signs and then Best picked up his saddle, jerking his head at Lucien to follow.

They saddled their horses and set off down the canyon to the level ground but instead of turning out towards the open desert, Best led the way along the canyon bottom through the mountains.

'This is the way that warrior and your sis went to miss the Apaches. They turned away from them. Now, they're up in the hills, here.'

After a while he dismounted and poked at something on the canyon floor with his finger. When he came back he was wiping his hand on a palmful of sand, and he climbed back into the saddle.

'I thought they was afoot,' he said. 'But them there horse apples was fresh. I dunno how they got mounts in the middle of the night, and I'd swear they didn't get any horses from the corral past me, awake or asleep.'

Lucien started to ask where did the horse dung come from, then realized it could only have come from the pursuing Apaches who were therefore now between them and their quarry. The question was, did the Apaches know that they were being followed? If so, was there time to catch them before they caught Emma and her captor?

Best hurried their pace, and Lucien found his pony beginning to labour. A tough little beast, it would go all day at its own pace, but its shorter legs were having to do the same work as the big mustang, and the pace was telling.

Just as he was about to ask for a break, Best pulled up and climbed down again, dropping on one knee to examine the ground, and then swore.

'What is it?' asked Lucien, dropping from his own horse to look at whatever Best had found. It was little enough: a few scrapes on a bulbous rock at the side of the trail, and a half seen hoofprint to one side.

'I think they're catching up on your sister and her beau,' Best explained. 'Until now, I wasn't sure the Apaches even knew about them two ahead of them, but they obviously do. They turned aside to follow them.'

Lucien was sweating with anxiety about his sister. Twice now he had been within reach of her, only to have her snatched away, and now he was chasing

Apaches who were chasing her.

'What is it about that girl?' he asked himself. 'What has she got?'

A little further on, he found out. She had got a fatal attraction. The proof was lying beside the trail, with no scalp and a broken arrow through its chest. The sentry from the Pima camp at the canyon had not made it to safety.

'Now we really have to hurry,' Best said. 'They got her again, and they think they got all the time in the world.'

He swung back into his saddle.

'They think,' he added, and urged the animal onwards. He pulled the Winchester from the saddle boot and flicked the action to send a shell into the chamber. Emma Wheatley needed them now more than ever, and Best was determined she would not need in vain.


They caught up with the Apaches only a couple of hours later. They were riding in single file along the bottom of a shallow canyon, and the girl was on a spare horse in the middle of their line, a horse which had paint on its haunches and a feather hanging from its bridle.

'Where did they get the horse?' Lucien wondered, as they lay along the crest of the ridge off to one side and watched the party.

'We provided them with it, when we shot the owner,' Best told him, focusing his field glasses on the girl's face. Her bodice had been badly ripped, and her shoulders were bare. She looked weary and

dirty, though to his surprise she did not look frightened. Every now and again in the glass he could see
her eyes flicker from side to side, though she kept
her head down in what must have looked like a
submissive posture.

'That girl's getting ready to run for it,' he told
Lucien out of the side of his mouth.

The boy nodded. 'She would be. Em don't behave
herself for nobody,' he said. There was a wealth of
pride in his voice.

Best noticed that the girl might have a dirty face
and her clothes might be torn and ragged, but she
sat astride her horse well, despite the lack of stirrups.
Her hands were not tied, and she was holding the
bridle of the pony as though she had been using an
Indian bridle all her life. The pony was only
restrained by a lead rein held by one of the warriors.

'She help you with the horses, boy?' he asked,
handing over the glasses.

'She certainly did,' Lucien said, steadying the
glasses with his elbows tucked into his ribs. 'Claims
she's a better rider than me!'

'That true?'

Lucien snorted, paused, and then said in a slightly
surprised voice, 'Probably is, come to think on it! She
can generally stay on anything this side of a wildcat,
and I ain't too sure about those. She ain't tried one,
recent.'

Best thought she probably could, if she put her
mind to it, and decided to gamble on it. Moving carefully to avoid raising dust, he led the horses along the
canyon out of sight of the Apaches, and prayed they

were not trailing any scouts. He had not seen any so far, though since they were Apaches he would probably not.

The canyon was coming to an end. The walls, never high, were coming down lower and lower, and the heads of the mounted men would be above the rim within a hundred yards. The warriors began to look around restlessly.

Emma judged her moment with a delicate precision. Just at the time when the Apaches' attention was distracted, she reached down and pulled up her petticoat to show that tucked into the top of her knee-high moccasins was a knife. In one fast movement, she whipped it out, and slashed through the lead rein that kept her following the warrior in front.

The Indian pony automatically shied aside as the bright steel flashed past his eyes, and the girl slapped her heels into his ribs and sent him in a series of bucking leaps up the side of the draw. The Apaches in front and behind her were caught by surprise, but reacted with venomous speed.

But the surprise had cost them a couple of seconds, and in that couple of seconds, she was at the top of the draw and starting down the other side.

Over the lip of the rise, she found herself confronted by her brother and Best crouching with their horses lying sideways in the sand. Both men had rifles to their shoulders and as the pursuing Apaches came over the lip of the draw in their turn, they took out the first two warriors. A third Indian, following slightly behind the first two, ran into a shot from Best's Colt and went backwards over the tail of his pony as though he had run into a bridge.

There were startled yells from the draw, but by the time they had cautiously scouted the ridge, the fugitives were half a mile away and going like jackrabbits with their tails on fire.

The Apaches boiled out of the draw and started their pursuit across the broken ground. They had several burning reasons for wanting, desperately, to catch up with the fugitives, starting with the fact that their surprise attack on the Pimas' cliff refuge had been humiliatingly rebuffed, and that their white woman captive had simply ridden out of their clutches and into freedom with her own people.

Three warriors had died in as many seconds. Their raid had crossed paths with other Apaches from a different group, always a recipe for accidents, and the accidents had happened.

They had lost blood, they had lost their captive, and they had lost their pride.

And as the high, clear notes of a US Cavalry bugle sounding a sickeningly familiar call filled the desert air, they had lost their chance for revenge.

Seething with resentment and hurt pride, they turned away to the south, yelling derisive insults at the approaching long-knife soldiers. There would be time, another day, to take their revenge.

# CHAPTER FOURTEEN

The command which came straggling over the ridge was the most tattered, shamefaced looking bunch of recruits Best had ever laid eyes on. Their hats were caked in white dust, their clothing so layered in it that they looked like statues.

Behind the main patrol came two led horses with blanket wrapped bodies roped over their saddles like bundles of rags – bundles which stank and plainly spooked the horses they burdened.

In front was the now familiar figure of Lieutenant Carey, a scarecrow now, the once smart uniform sadly worn and tattered, but the eternal sabre bright and shining in the sun, a blazing blade of light resting on his shoulder.

Sergeant O'Mahoney was riding a few paces behind him still, but a very different O'Mahoney now. His campaign hat had been slashed across the brim, which hung in a loop over his ear. There was blood on the shoulder of his shirt, and he was favouring his right arm, holding the reins in his left hand and keeping his right tucked into the front of his belt.

He had been in the wars and he looked it. So did the rest of the patrol.

Best pulled up his horse and waited for the force to come down to him. It took longer than it should because of the horses' obvious exhaustion, but they came.

Carey pulled up when he was in front of them and looked them over as though he were reviewing punishment parade.

'Sergeant O'Mahoney!' he snapped in a voice rusty with dust and exhaustion.

'Sir!' O'Mahoney looked as though he were staying in his saddle only by an effort of will, and a desperate one, at that.

'Put these men under arrest! And identify that Indian woman immediately!'

Best stared at the sergeant, and the sergeant stared back at him, and mind spoke to mind across the rocks.

'Best!' said O'Mahoney. 'You are under arrest!'

'Oh, no I ain't,' Best told him flatly.

There was a short silence. Carey turned his head and then his whole body to face Best.

'What did this man say?' he asked.

'He says he ain't, sir,' O'Mahoney told him.

The officer stared at him for a second, and then kicked his horse into action. Just what he intended to do, Best could not guess but he had taken enough from this madman.

'You come near me with that pig-sticker, mister, and I will blow your goddam' head clean to Fort Whipple,' he said, loudly and clearly. Whether Carey was actually understanding much of what he heard, Best could not guess, but he reckoned the man could comprehend the drawn Colt.

Carey stopped his horse and stared around him. None of the troopers had moved at all, and several were not even looking at him. One had unfastened his blanket from behind his saddle and offered it to Emma. She accepted it gratefully and threw it around her shoulders. Odd, thought Best irrelevantly, that when in the company of the Indians she had been apparently unaware of her bare shoulders and dirty face, but as soon as white men turned up, who would understand and have sympathy with her state of undress, she became self-conscious.

O'Mahoney stared from Best to Carey and then to the girl. For some reason the discovery that they had found the kidnapped woman seemed to jolt him into reality.

'Pardon me, ma'am, but are you Miss Wheatley?' he said.

She stopped scrubbing at her face with the corner of the borrowed blanket and stared at him.

'Well, of course I am,' she said. 'Who did you think I was? Boadicea?'

There was, miraculously, a splutter of laughter among the troopers. One or two of them, in the presence of a white woman, began slapping the dust from their uniforms and punching their hats into some form of shape.

Best did not dare take his eyes off the demented officer, but Carey, once he had been faced down with a revolver, seemed to have relapsed into his other-worldly trance. He sat upright on his horse, with the sword resting against his shoulder and surveyed the surrounding hills with his field-glasses.

O'Mahoney dismounted the men, and set sentries, then arranged some shelter for the girl with blankets hanging over a couple of rocks. Best contributed a shirt for her, and one of the men contrived a hat out of bandannas. Water was taken from their canteens so that she could at least have enough to scrub her hands and face.

A fire was lit and coffee made.

The woman who appeared from the contrived shelter, head bound in a turban and shoulders covered with Best's shirt, belted tightly with a length of line, was a totally different proposition from the grubby, tattered figure who had entered it.

One of the troopers gave a low whistle and was instantly the focus of a barrage of outraged frowns.

'Thank you all very much for all your kind contributions,' she said, smiling round the circle of admiring faces. 'It is so kind of you to look after me so well.'

A rumble of murmured protests sounded. Shucks, it weren't nothing, ma'am. Glad to be able to be of assistance, little lady. Think nothin' of it, please. Booted feet shuffled, even more dust was pounded out of their battered hats and uniforms.

Carey showed some awareness of his surroundings. He stared at Emma again, sheathed his sabre and dismounted to lead her to a rock where he seated her with the ceremony due to a duchess, and called for coffee.

Best cornered the sergeant.

'What the hell's been going on, Mick?' he asked. 'Last time I saw you, the whole caboodle of you was making for the fort. What are you doin' back up here?'

The big Irishman scrubbed at the inside of his hat with his bandanna and settled it on his head again. He looked totally exhausted, the lines cleft deep into his face and his eyes bloodshot with fatigue.

'Johnny, boy,' he said. 'I feel like I carried this lunatic and these here recruits all the way up from the Gila on my back. We bypassed chances to ride into Gila Bend and Vulture, and we could easily have stopped at Wagoner's. We're miles out of our patrol area, and we lost two boys on the way. That's them, stinking, back there and spooking the horses.'

Best stared at him. The O'Mahoney he knew was a tough, experienced professional soldier, a man who had fought his way through the War Between the States as a trooper, been decorated and promoted, and served in the south-west with distinction.

'Why didn't you just shoot the bastard and take these boys home?' he asked. The question was not serious, but the temptation must have been at the back of the sergeant's mind.

O'Mahoney wiped his hand down over his face.

'It wasn't just this damn fool,' he said. 'We been harried by the Apaches all the way up here. Hit and run, and the only time he makes a decision is to run after 'em!

'I can't refuse to attack the enemy, Johnny, you know that. Even when it's a waste of the lives of good men, I got no choice. You was jokin' about shooting the man, I know, but so help me, I come this close to

it over the past twenty-four hours. He's more dangerous than Geronimo.'

Best clapped him on the shoulder, and turned
back to the fire, where Emma was receiving the
devoted attention of the entire command, and enjoy-
ing every second of it. He was amazed at the girl's
resilience. She had seen her parents and family
killed, been kidnapped and he had no doubt cruelly
mistreated by the Apache, bartered to another group
of Indians, recaptured by the Apaches, and made a
dash for freedom.

She was, he thought, a remarkable woman. But
they needed to get her up to Whipple as soon as they
could. And that meant that O'Mahoney had to take
charge of the command, and they had to get under
way as soon as possible.

The horses, he noticed, were looking a great deal
better than when they arrived. They would take days
to get back to full health but they no longer looked
ready to drop in their tracks.

Whipple was a good day's march away, on healthy
strong beasts ridden by healthy strong men, and this
patrol looked like it needed ambulance wagons.

O'Mahoney shouted for coffee and two cups were
brought. Young Lucien was sitting with his sister and
benefiting from the attention she attracted. He
looked as though his brain was awash with coffee, and
his teeth showed a lot when he looked at his sister.
She was all the family he had got, now, and he looked
determined not to let her out of his sight again.

There was a spring to the north of them, and so was

150

the trail up Skull Valley which would take them into the post.

At Best's suggestion, O'Mahoney buried the two dead troopers under piles of stones, and the command stood bareheaded while the sergeant read a passage from his well thumbed Bible over the graves. Carey sat on his horse nearby with his sabre at the salute, occasionally issuing a crisp order which was ignored by the rest of the party by tacit agreement. A few sideways glances were thrown at him, but that was all.

Best was worried about the disappearance of the Apaches. They had not been defeated, merely driven off, and they knew that there was a woman with the command as well as the equipment the troopers carried, and whatever ammunition they had left.

Plenty of bait for an Apache with a gleam in his eye, and this bunch had been tormenting the troopers for days. Best cast progressively more worried glances at the crests of the hills and hillocks as they filed off towards Antelope Spring.

At the spring itself, surrounded by grass and a few cottonwoods, O'Mahoney let them water by pairs, and the water bottles were filled. Emma took the opportunity to wet her bandanna head-cloth and scrub her face and neck, before wrapping the wet cloth round her head to keep her cool.

The coming of night was lengthening the shadows rapidly when they left the water and headed on up the valley, and into the shade of the foothills. At O'Mahoney's request, Best led them into a cove above the trail, and they made camp with sentries set and the horses tethered within the group.

'What d'ye reckon?' O'Mahoney asked him as they hunkered down by a rock. The girl and her brother were securely tucked away under the overhang of the edge of the cove, and faint murmurs came from their pile of blankets. They must be comparing notes, Best reckoned.

He also reckoned they had both done well, for a pair of young people who had recently lost their family in horrific circumstances.

'About the kids? They'll do,' he said. 'About the Apaches? They're out there, and I reckon by daylight they're planning to be in here. Keep wakeful watch at first light. About me? I want to sleep for a week, but I will settle for two hours. Wake me and I'll scout before we leave.'

He rolled himself in his blankets and settled himself with his head against a rock. After a couple of seconds, the sergeant realized he was asleep, and did a round of the sentries. They were all awake, he was delighted to find, largely because they were more frightened of him than they were of the Indians.

Carey was sitting with his back against a rock, and his chin resting on the pommel of his sabre. He raised his head as O'Mahoney paused near him.

'Good man. Checking the sentries, are you? Good man. Sentries are very important in a hostile envi-ronment,' he said. O'Mahoney saluted smartly and wished the fool had stayed with his privileged family in Baltimore.

# CHAPTER FIFTEEN

The Apaches came over the rim of the cove in the pearly light just before the dawn, in a concerted rush.

First, Best noticed that the horses which were standing, heads down and packed together in the chill of the desert night, raised their heads, ears pricked, and looked towards the west rim of the cove. His own horse whickered gently and shifted its hoofs as though getting ready to run, and he grabbed at its halter and put his hands gently over its nose.

The nearest sentry was a raw recruit who had noticed nothing, but the man at the head of the cove was more desert wise and Best saw him glance at the horses and then cock his rifle, and look around, warily.

Best kicked at the feet of O'Mahoney, and the big Irishman came awake and to his feet in the same instant. He was cocking his rifle when the first warrior came over the rim of the cove with a yell like some demon from the pit, and suddenly, the whole area was over-run with yelling warriors.

Best saw one trooper go down as he tried to load his carbine, and another swinging his weapon like a battle axe. It connected with the skull of a charging Apache, and the warrior somersaulted into the remains of the night's fire.

The sentry who had been alerted by the horses was cocking and firing his Colt like an automaton, moving his aim methodically. He was holding his carbine in his left hand and swung it in a vicious horizontal arc as two Apaches went for him from opposite sides. The carbine connected, but the hammer of his pistol fell on an empty chamber and the Indian's axe bit into his shoulder.

At the far side of the cove, Emma was crouching behind her brother, her own back against a boulder, and a knife clutched in her hand, stabbing out at legs when she thought she could reach. Best saw her connect at least once, and Lucien was making spirited play with his clubbed carbine above her head.

For a few minutes, the cove was a seething pit of struggling men and trampling, squealing horses, and then, as suddenly as they had come, the Indians were gone. Behind them, they left two dead soldiers and one with his left arm immobilized from a stab wound. The horses gradually calmed down and stopped trampling around.

Best glanced over at the officer and swore incredulously. The man was still sitting by his rock, leaning his chin on his reversed sabre and staring dreamily at the ashes of a ruined fire by his feet. He seemed to be unhurt, indeed, unmoved by the maelstrom of violence which had filled the cove. His lips were pursed and as the horses calmed down, Best realized the man was whistling under his breath.

O'Mahoney was organizing a firing step at the mouth of the cove, and one by one, sending the troopers to saddle their calming horses.

Best saddled his own mount and passed it a lump of sugar he had been hoarding in his saddle bag. The horse crunched it delicately, and nuzzled him for more.

'Later, boy,' he told it, stroking its nose. 'You can have a pound loaf to yourself when we get back to the post.'

*If* we get back to the post, he told himself, and then was ashamed of himself for the thought. Of course they were going to get back, and that young woman and her brother were going to get back with them.

O'Mahoney had a couple of his men pull the dead troopers to the edge of the cove and empty their pockets. The contents, wrapped in their bandannas, were passed to him and he pushed them into his saddlebags. Ordinarily it would be the duty of the officer commanding to return their valuables to their families where possible, with a letter of condolence, but in this case, the sergeant thought glumly, it would be him.

'Here they come again, Sergeant!' shouted the lookout at the mouth of the cove, and the Apaches came, this time on horseback, whirling past the mouth of the makeshift fort refuge and firing in as they came.

Best hastily looked at the other end of the cove, and caught another group of warriors as they came over the edge, in an attempt to catch the soldiers from behind while their attention was distracted.

His shout of warning coincided with Lucien's yell,

and the bang of his carbine, and Emma screamed like a banshee. The Apaches were caught halfway down the wall of the cove, and two fell limply down into the floor before they could get back up the steep slope.

The attack fizzled out. A wounded horse was squealing and thrashing its hoofs until one of the troopers leaned dangerously close and shot it in the head with his revolver.

'Right!' shouted O'Mahoney. 'Wounded all bandaged? Mount up! We're going out and north, and I'll shoot the first man who tries to drop out. Wounded and the bodies go with us!'

The troopers went out of the cove like an avalanche, whooping like Indians themselves, and thundered up the valley to the north. Out among the rocks, there was a spattering of fire but the charge seemed to have caught the Apaches by surprise, and their own mounted men had apparently dismounted and left their horses somewhere out of range. At any rate, there was no immediate pursuit, and the soldiers, cloaked in a cloud of dust, swept past them and off up the valley.

It was not until they stopped to tend to the wounded that anybody noticed that Carey was dead. He was still sitting on his horse, knees clamped like a strangler's hands, his sabre still resting on his shoulder. Where his left eye should have been was a hole and when they took the body down from the saddle, they realized that only his tightly jammed kepi was keeping his brains in place.

The men stared at him and then at one another in amazement and one of them swore, fluently and foully. O'Mahoney shouted him into silence, glancing nervously at the girl, but she seemed unmoved by the outburst. Like the others she was simply amazed that the officer had stayed on his horse.

In the end, they did not even know when he had died. Simply that he was alive when they charged out of the little gulch and dead when they lifted him down from the saddle. It took two of them to prise his hand from the hilt of his sword, and return it to its scabbard.

His death seemed somehow to have released the command from a spell. Men who had avoided one another's eyes started to talk animatedly. Instead of riding with their shoulders hunched uneasily, they started to look round them with sharpened awareness. They came, in short, to life again.

O'Mahoney showed the most change. The discovery of the kidnapped girl had already awakened his interest, and now he was back almost to his old, confident self. He stopped referring to Best for advice and issued his orders without a glance over his shoulder, and tongue lashed the command back into alert awareness.

Twice, they saw dust on their back trail. Twice, O'Mahoney halted the party and formed a line with the horses securely penned behind them, and scouts out to give early warning. Twice, the dust settled and no attack developed.

By dusk, they were riding into the gates of Fort Whipple, a dusty tired body of men on dusty, tired horses with their dead and their spare horses trailing behind them.

Best peeled off, and took Lucien and his sister to the MO's office, where the post doctor, a thin, desiccated man with nose like a sharp beak and eyes as beady as a hunting buzzard, took them into his surgery and slammed the door in Best's face.

'Go wash up and see to your mount, man,' he snapped, when Best protested. 'You can come back when you smell more like a human being and less like a shippon.'

Dr Carter was an Englishman and delighted in using the vocabulary of his North Country youth. He left the door closed for a long count of five, then snatched it open again.

'It's a cattle shed, numbskull. You smell like a cattle shed. One that hasn't been mucked out lately, too. Go and bathe.'

Best sniffed at his shirt, new from the shelves of the store at Vulture less than a week ago, and acknowledged the crusty old medico had a point. By the time he came back, fresh from the tub at the back of the bunkhouse, and wearing yet another new shirt and his own clean jeans, the young people were sitting on the stoop outside the MO's quarters and drinking lemonade from tall glasses.

'Clean bill of health for these two – in fact, they're in top condition,' reported Carter who also had a glass, but plainly not of lemonade. He took a long drag on his cigar and blew out a long plume of smoke into the still evening air. It hung, like a bad conscience, over his head until he waved it away impatiently.

'My good lady has arranged quarters for them at

the back, here. Hospital's empty at the moment, and she needs something to do,' he said. 'The colonel's going to see them in the morning, but what they need most of all is sleep and some good food inside them. You can join us for dinner, and we can talk later.'

The dinner was good, and the Wheatleys were bundled off to bed despite their protests that they were not children and not tired, and Best sat on the stoop in his turn with the doctor, and cradled a glass.

'Both their parents dead, I gather, and the rest of their family, too. Tragic tale, and only too common,' said the doctor when the cigars had been lit. Best nodded and sipped at the whiskey. It was bourbon, and the doctor was famous for it, though he dispensed it sparingly.

'So what's going to happen to these two?' said the doctor. 'They don't seem to have any surviving relations, though they are Mormons, and I have no doubt the Saints will take them in, if asked.'

As servants maybe. Not as relations, and certainly not without working for their keep. The girl in particular would have to put up with a lot of sly looks and nudges. The lot of a woman returned from captivity with the Indians was notoriously hard.

'What did the CO say?' he asked. The doctor tapped the ash from the end of his cigar and pursed his lips.

'Says he'll put them on the strength. The boy can sign up when he's older, or train as a trumpeter now, and the girl can be a laundress. Hard life, but she'll get her rations and accommodation, and the post ladies will keep a friendly enough eye on her.'

The young people could do a great deal worse. Here at least they would be protected and provided for. The post ladies were a tough lot, but they looked after their own well enough.

'Did you ask them about it?' he asked, sipping from the glass. 'What do they think? They may have ideas of their own.'

The surgeon gave a cough of laughter and leaned across the table to tap him on the chest.

'Oh, they have ideas of their own, all right. At any rate that very attractive young lady has. The first thing she asked me was if you were married or keeping company with any of the ladies of the fort.'

'What?' Best shot upright and stared.

'And the second thing was how big is a scout's accommodation, and would it fit a married man and his family.' He gave another harsh bark of amusement and leaned back.

'Were I you, I would think about taking to the hills, young Best. That girl's got her sights plumb dead centre on you, and she doesn't look like a young lady who is liable to miss what she aims at!'

He would not stop laughing all evening, and by the time he went off to his own quarters, Best found himself considering how much more cheerful they would look with a woman's touch to cheer them up.

'She's darned pretty, too!' he told his horse, as he bedded it down for the night, and the bay blew through its nose and seemed to nod agreement.